*To my young Tyneside friends,
Iain and Paul Nicholson*

1

'Look, Ma, I can see to meself and our Penny.'

Lilian Morley placed one hand over her mouth and the other on her chest as she coughed a number of times; then looked up into her son's stiff face, at his ruffled black hair and round dark brown eyes, and she drew in a deep painful breath before she acknowledged, 'I haven't the slightest doubt that you could take care of yourself, Eddie; but you can't take care of Penny at the same time' – she now pointed to her daughter, who was sitting by the side of the open grate, her head turned towards the fire – 'You won't be here when she comes home from school.'

'Good gracious, Ma, she's not a bairn; and we're not living in the dark ages, it's 1890 remember; she can take the key and turn it in the lock, can't she?' he demanded, thrusting his hand out towards the door.

'And what about when you go to the Institute in the evening for your engineering class? Were you thinking of giving that up?' His mother's voice now had an unusually harsh note in it, and his head drooped for a moment before it jerked upwards again and he cried, 'Yes, I can, I can give it up. You're only goin' to be away three months, I can soon catch up, I can work here at home. Mr Leonard will give me the books.'

The mother and son stared hard at each other now. Then Mrs Morley, turning towards her daughter, said, 'Take sixpence out of the jug, Penny, and go and get a loaf and three sugar buns.'

The young girl rose slowly from the chair and, keeping her face averted from them, went to the end of the fireplace, reached up, and lifted the jug from the mantelpiece. She took from it a sixpence; then still with face averted, she went from the room and out of the door which led straight into the front street.

Hardly had the door closed on her before Eddie, bending towards his mother and whispering now as if he might be overheard, said, 'She's bubbling, not just because you're going away, Ma, it's because she doesn't want to go to Gran-Flan's.'

Mrs Morley closed her eyes for a moment, then she said quietly, 'Sit down, Eddie.'

It seemed as if Eddie were reluctant to obey his mother's command, but after hesitating he swung a plain wooden chair round from under the table and, sitting down, folded his arms across his chest and stared at his mother.

'Have you ever thought how pretty your sister is?' Mrs Morley said softly now.

Eddie screwed up his eyes as he asked, 'What's that to do with it, Ma?'

'Everything, Eddie. You know what kind of quarter we live in, don't you, and round the corner is Thornton Avenue? And as you know it's full of lodging houses, mostly occupied by foreign sailors. And just a bit further on is the docks proper with all those bars facing it. A decent body isn't able to pass along there at night without almost tripping over sprawling, drunken men. And you know I have never let Penny play on the streets after dark like the other children round the doors.

'Now, Eddie,' – she slowly shook her head – 'I'm asking you to imagine what would happen if she was her own. Even inside this house she wouldn't be safe, because things get about. People know I've been ill and that I'm going away. Anyone with bad intentions could knock at that door, and she would open it ... You see what I mean?'

Eddie's head slowly drooped. 'Yes.' He could see now what his mother meant. He hadn't worked in the docks for the past eighteen months with his ears closed. Men talked about things, they laughed about things, yes, he could see his mother's point of view. Yet he didn't want to go and live at his Granny Flannagan's, not even for three months; three months was a lifetime.

'I'll go mad staying in that house, Ma. It's right off the beaten track, and you can even hear the sea beating against the rocks when you're in the house. But the worst thing of all is havin' to put up with Gran-Flan and her bloomin' ear trumpet. It's worse than being in the shipyards, the noise you've got to make to get yourself understood.'

His mother smiled weakly and said quietly,

'You've never understood your granny. And I wish you wouldn't call her Gran-Flan.'

'I'll call her what I like,' Eddie said, rising to his feet and thrusting the chair aside. 'As for understanding her, did she understand me da?' Turning towards his mother again and his voice a shout, he demanded, 'And did she understand you when you married him? No, she threw you out.'

'She didn't throw me out.'

'Well, it was as good as; you couldn't take me da back to the house. And why? Because he was a *common* man, a docker.'

'He wasn't a common man to me; and he was a gaffer in the docks. Remember that.'

'Aw, Ma!' Impatiently now, Eddie shook his head from side to side. 'He rose to be a gaffer later, but when you married him he was an iron ore man. And he was never ashamed of it. Aw, don't cry, Ma. I'm sorry, I'm sorry. Look, you'll bring on an attack.'

As his mother's breathing became agitated with the asthma, he went hastily to her and put his arm about her shoulders, and as he patted her, he said, in a conciliatory tone now, 'I'm ... I'm proud of me da. He was well respected, well liked. The men still talk about him. Wouldn't do a man out of a farthing, they say; and he never docked their time. He knew how they felt and thought 'cos he'd had to go through the same thing, workin' ten hours in the holds, wet up to the thighs when they had to dig out the ore from the wet clay, and all for three and sixpence a shift. He understood them.' He paused; then, his voice

10

falling away, he added, 'He understood everybody.'

He straightened up and walked to the fireplace, and reaching out to the brass rod that ran underneath the mantelshelf, he pushed the towels aside that were hanging there and gripped the rod. Then bending his head, he looked down into the fire and said, 'I'll never like me granny, not until the day I die, for she never gave him a hearing. She could never see the man he was, she could only see the dirty job he had to do.'

There followed a silence in the kitchen, broken only by the sound of a cart and horse on the cobbled street outside, until he swung round and, his voice now so loud it startled his mother, he cried, 'All right, I'll go. Without further ado I'll go. But I bet by the end of three months she'll be more glad to see the back of me than I shall of her. And that's a promise, Ma.'

'Come here.' She held out her hand to him. And it was with seeming reluctance that he went towards her again, and when she gripped his hand between her own two, she looked up into his face for some seconds before saying, 'There's one thing I'm happy about, your father will never be dead as long as you're alive;' and gripping his hand tightly now, she added, 'I won't know a minute's peace if you're not settled in before I go.'

'How do you know I'll stay there, Ma? How do you know I won't do a flit and come back here once you're out of the way?'

'You'll stay there. Didn't I say you're like your father? You said you'd go and you'll go, and you'll see it through.'

As she nodded confirmation of her words he withdrew his hand from hers and went towards the door that led into the only other room of the house; but as he lifted the latch, he turned and, looking at her over his shoulder, he said, 'Has it struck you, Ma, that I'll have to walk almost three miles each way to work?'

'Yes, it has, Eddie. But then I didn't give much attention to that part of it seeing that it's your favourite boast you can do ten to fifteen miles on a Sunday without a blister.'

Eddie drew in a long breath, pushed open the door, then shut it none too gently behind him before crossing to the window.

Standing with his hands on the sill, he looked into the little square of backyard with its wash-house that was shared with the upstairs tenants, the two dry lavatories, and the two coal houses, and it was as if he were looking on to a beautiful garden, so great was his reluctance to leave this house in which he had been born and brought up.

Things weren't fair, there was injustice some-where, everywhere really. Why had his father to go and drop down dead two years ago? He was only thirty-eight years old and looked as strong as a horse. They said his heart gave out, but he used to thump his bare chest and take in deep breaths that expanded it four inches. Now if it had been his mother it would have been under-standable, because she'd always had a weak chest. Bronchial they called it, bronchial asthma. She couldn't get her breath at times, and since his father had died it had become worse and worse.

He supposed he should be glad she had been given the chance to go to this place up in Northumberland, Hexham way. It was a big house on a hill, so he was told, and it was good for people with her complaint.

He might have looked at things differently if everything hadn't been arranged by his granny. It was funny, when he came to think about it, but he had only known his granny for two years, in fact since his father died. He had heard about her indirectly through listening to his ma and da talking at night. He could remember his da getting angry and his ma pleading with him, very likely to go along to see the old vixen. He was glad, oh yes, he was glad his da hadn't given in.

But it was long before his father died that he had seen his granny's house, the place where his mother was born. Rock End they called it, and it was well named for it was perched high on top of the cliff with not a house or habitation in sight either way you looked. He had made it his business to go past it on one of his Sunday jaunts. There was a garden, or what should have been a garden around three sides of it, but it was so overgrown it looked like a jungle. In front of it, on the sea side, was grassland, and this ran level for about the size of a good paddock before sloping steeply towards the cliff edge.

He had come into closer acquaintance with that slope the first time he visited the house. It was after a letter had come from his granny, when his mother had taken him and Penny on their first visit.

The visits had become numerous, more so over

the past few months, and with each one the dislike of his granny had grown, if that was possible. Yet he didn't mind his grandfather. In a way he felt sorry for him because Gran-Flan seemed to have him under her thumb. And look at the way she worked Daisy Clinton, and her only a bit of a lass, just a year or so older than Penny. But then he hadn't to forget that Daisy Clinton could take care of herself. She was pert, and cheeky. Oh aye, she was cheeky all right.

And then there was Mr Kemp, Hal Kemp. His ma said they had to call him Uncle Hal. He disliked him almost as much as he disliked his granny.

He turned abruptly from the window now and went to a chest-of-drawers, the top drawer of which he pulled open. From it he grabbed his clean linen and almost in the same movement threw it onto the bed. Then he set about parcelling up the belongings he would need for the next week or so. Only once did he stop his rough bustling to and fro; it was when a thought entered his mind, and the thought was like a voice speaking to him as it said, 'You never disliked or hated anybody until your da died.' And he listened to the voice for a moment before he answered it, saying, 'Well, I hadn't met me granny then, had I?'

2

'Look, we haven't time to stop stall gazing.'

With a jerk of his head Eddie beckoned Penny away from the market stall which appeared to hold every variety of boiled sweet that had ever been manufactured; and when she came to his side she looked up at him and said, 'I'd like to spend some of me threepence.'

'Well, there's no time, we've got more than a mile to go afore we get to the sands and the cart, and we'll be lucky if we get to the house afore dark. Anyway, you want to hang on to your money, you never know when you'll need it.'

What was he talking about? What use was threepence! Why couldn't he let her buy some taffie?

'Go on' – he pushed her now – 'don't take all day.'

As he waited for her to be served at the stall he looked about him, at the milling crowds that filled the market. He loved the smell of the market, but as strong as the smell was it could never wholly blanket down the smell of the river just beyond it, the river that was alive with life, ships from all over the world sailing up and down it,

15

and its banks covered with yards of all descriptions, mostly connected with the making of ships, iron ships. Everything was iron and steel now. But he liked iron and steel; they were the materials of an engineer. And that's what he would be one day. By! aye, if he had any say in it he'd be an engineer, qualified, with a certificate from technical school . . .

'Look! Eddie, I've got a haporth of cinder taffie and a haporth of everlasting stripes; and those are for you, tiger nuts.' She pushed a bag into his hand, and he looked at it for a moment before weighing it and saying, 'There's more than a haporth here.'

'There's a pennorth.' She turned away from him as she picked out a piece of cinder taffie from a cornet shaped bag that had been fashioned out of a square of newspaper.

'You shouldn't have spent a whole penny.'

She turned a bright face up to him now and pursed her lips before retorting, 'Well, I did. And I bet, knowin' you and tiger nuts, there won't be any left when we get to me granny's.'

As he smiled widely at her now his face seemed transformed. The dark, sombre look that it had worn all day was momentarily replaced by a twinkling merriment, made partly self-conscious by the fact of his weakness for tiger nuts. Stuffing the bag of nuts into his coat pocket, he nudged her with his elbows, saying, 'Come on.'

As they made their way towards King Street, Penny moved the neatly wrapped parcel of her clothes she was carrying from one arm to the other as she said, 'This is getting heavy. Do you think we could take the horse tram?'

'What!' His pleasant expression vanished. 'Who do you think we are, millionaires? Anyway, when we get to the bottom of Ocean Road, Hal should be there with the cart, that's if he's remembered to pull himself out of a pub.'

'Why don't you call him Uncle Hal?'

'Because he's not me uncle, he's me granny's brother's son. That makes him me ma's cousin, so how can he be me uncle?'

Penny was dragging her feet somewhat when they came to the end of Ocean Road and within sight of a neat looking small flat cart and an equally neat looking horse.

A man was leaning against the side of the cart. He was of medium build but muscular; his neck was short and thick, making his head appear to be set in his shoulders. His hair sticking out from the sides of his hard hat was brown, and his face was of a ruddy hue. His features were not unpleasant, except that one eye was noticeably smaller than the other, but this gave an odd, merry quirk to his face.

But his voice belied his expression as he hailed them with, 'Well, you've got here then! You've taken your time. What do you think I am, a foot-man with your carriage and pair?'

Eddie didn't answer him but Penny, in a conciliatory tone, put in, 'It's a long way, Uncle Hal.'

'It's a long way, Uncle Hal,' the man mimicked her now as, bending down, he put his hands under her oxters and lifted her up onto the back of the cart. There, still holding her, he put his face close

17

to hers and again said, 'It's a long way, Uncle Hal.' And at this she laughed nervously.

'You said half-past four and it is half-past four.' Eddie had thrown both parcels on to the cart and was now holding in his hand a big gold-cased lever watch.

Slowly Hal Kemp turned his attention on to him and the watch and he jerked his chin up as he said, 'My! my! we are somebody, aren't we, supporting a gold lever? Where did you pinch that?'

'It was me father's.' The words came slow and distinct, and Penny, hitching herself back on the cart, said nervously, 'Come on, our Eddie, come on, get yourself up.'

Eddie had called their da, father. Whenever he spoke like that it always meant he was angry inside. Her voice high now, she cried at him, 'Our Eddie! come on, me granny'll be waiting.'

Eddie snapped the case of the watch closed, put it in his pocket, gave one last look at the man, then hoisted himself on to the back of the cart, and within a minute or two they moved off.

They travelled by the sea road for some distance. To the left of them was the famous, or infamous, Herd Sands where so many boats had been wrecked and so many lives had been lost, and in sight too of the helpless watchers on the shore. Presently, veering right, they went along a rough track bordered by green fields; then, when almost opposite the Trow Rocks, they turned towards the cliff tops again. Away to the left of them was Trow Point, and close by Graham's Sand.

Now the track seemed almost to touch the edge

of the cliff as it neared Frenchman's Bay and although in fact it was still a good many yards from the actual edge, Penny put out her hand towards Eddie, and he, taking it, shook his head at her, signifying there was nothing to be afraid of.

Once past the point where the coast line penetrated furthest inland, the track, as if tired of travelling along the edge of the cliff turned abruptly away and dropped into a shallow valley, and when they had ridden up the other side of the valley there in the distance was the house, and to Eddie it looked as uninviting now as on the first occasion he had seen it.

Even from a distance it looked a long low house. It was two-storied and built of stone, with a slate roof. Its name, Rock End, signified strength, and it had lived up to it for the past hundred and twenty years, for the North Sea, which pounded the foot of the rocks on which it was built, battered it with its storms and deafened its occupants at least half the year with its thunder. For the rest of the time it made itself heard using different voices according to its moods.

Hal Kemp turned the cart into the yard that ran by the side of the house. The yard was bordered by a stable, a coal house, a wood store, and a wash-house. The wash-house wall adjoined that of the kitchen quarters, the door into which was noticeable in that it was in two halves, like that of the stable.

As they dismounted, the top half of the door was pulled open to show young Daisy Clinton's pert face topped by a mass of fair hair. But she did not attempt to open the lower half of the door until Eddie and Penny were standing on the other side, and then, her face one large beam, she said, 'Look what the tide's washed up! Well, don't stand there, come on in if you don't want the wind to cut the nose off your face.' And on this she quickly pulled open the lower half of the door and ushered them into the kitchen.

'Here! give me your bundles.' She grabbed the parcels from their arms and, throwing them on to a wooden settle that was set at right angles to a huge black-leaded range with a fire burning brightly in the middle of it, supplying heat to the oven at one side and a water boiler at the other, she now turned to them again and with the flat of her hand she pushed Penny in the chest, saying, 'Eeh! it's nice to see you, and you gona stay.' Then flicking her bright gaze to Eddie, she looked into his straight face and said, 'Hello, you.'

Eddie could say that he liked Daisy, she was all right – for a girl – except at times, like now, when she had the habit of acting as if she were older than him, which annoyed him and made him want to put her in her place – sort of. But how did one go about it with someone like Daisy? Now if it had been Penny, or another lad.

He was thinking up some sharp retort when Hal Kemp entered the kitchen and, going straight to the fire, stood with his back to it. Then bending slightly forward, he lifted up the back of his reefer jacket and rubbed his buttocks vigorously with the palms of his hands as he said, 'Well now, here we are, delivered all safe and sound.

And I hope you know how lucky you are.' He seemed to be addressing himself particularly to Eddie, and he ended, ' 'Tisn't everybody that's taken from the slums into a house like this to be looked after and . . .'

'What do you mean, slums?' Eddie's neck was stretching upwards, his chin thrust out. 'We never lived in the slums. And this happens to be me grandfather's and grandmother's house, so who has more right to be here, eh?'

'Well, I'll be damned! you cheeky young snot.' Hal Kemp moved slowly from the fire towards the long kitchen table on which were two large trays piled high with tea crockery and surrounded by plates of food. Leaning his hands flat on it he looked across it towards Eddie and, his head now nodding slowly, he said, 'I'd watch me tongue, young man, if I was you. You've hardly got your foot inside the door and you're claiming ownership.'

'I'm doin' no such thing, I'm merely sayin' if it comes to the point we've got as much right here as anybody else.'

They stared at each other fixedly now. Then Hal Kemp, turning his head to the side and his eyes widening, nodded towards Daisy, saying, 'Did you ever hear the likes of it? I ask you! Do you see what we're in for? We're a peaceable family, all of us together, at least we were, but I can tell you this much, Daisy, them days are gone.'

Daisy's face was unsmiling now and her voice quiet as she said, 'I don't think he meant any harm, Mr Hal.'

21

'I hope you're right, Daisy, I hope you're right for all our sakes.' And on this he nodded at her as he buttoned up his coat and walked to the door and out into the yard again.

'Eeh!' Daisy's voice was a mere whisper now. 'You've got on the wrong side of him. Why had you to go an' cheek him?'

'I didn't cheek him, I simply told him the truth. And who is he anyway? Me ma said nobody had heard of him for twenty years until a year ago. Anyway, whoever he is' – Eddie's chin jerked from side to side now – 'he's not gona get the better of me . . . Where's me granny and granda?'

'They're in the parlour.'

'Come on.' Eddie now thrust Penny before him and walked down the length of the long, narrow kitchen and through a door and into a dim square hall that looked at first glance as if it might be the cabin of a sailing ship for where the wall space wasn't taken up with doors it was covered with glass cases in which were models of all types of ships, old men of war, whalers, passenger ships, tugs, keels, and even little scullers. The floor was of stone and covered here and there with rope mats.

Opposite the parlour door they stopped and glanced at each other for a moment before Eddie turned the handle and went in.

It would have been no use knocking for his granny couldn't hear him, and on the occasions when he had been here before, his grandfather had been asleep in the big leather chair.

The difference between the parlour and the hall was striking in that the room was light, even though the twilight was deepening. Moreover, the atmosphere was one of homely comfort.

As he expected, his grandfather was asleep in his chair. Whether his grandmother was awake or asleep, he couldn't tell, for she had her back to them. But when she made a movement in the chair he guessed she was awake all right.

Going ahead of Penny now, he skirted the little round table on which lay her black hearing trumpet, and then he was standing in front of her and marvelling once again that anyone so small and thin, and who looked so old, could contain inside themselves such a voice as hers.

'Hello, Gran.' He made his lips move widely as he shouted the words.

'Oh, there you are! You're late. I expected you this afternoon.' Her big, round faded brown eyes set in their wrinkled pouches looked from him to Penny, then back again as she bawled now, 'Well! don't stand there like a johnny-cum-canny, get your things off. That's if you're going to stay.'

'W . . . hat! What! Oh . . . hello . . . hello there.' They turned to see their grandfather sitting up in his chair rubbing the sleep from his eyes, and they both said, 'Hello, Granda.'

'Aw, it's nice to see you.' The old man put one arm out and drew Penny towards him, and he extended his other hand towards Eddie, saying, 'Well, well, now, isn't this nice! But . . . but come on, get your things off . . .'

Before he had finished the last word, Granny Flannagan bellowed loudly, 'You gona eat and sleep in those clothes? Now get your coats off, and out of those boots and into slippers. You don't get past the hall in boots. Remember that . . .'

'Where's that girl!' She now screwed around in her chair. 'The tea should have been ready ages ago. Don't stand there, boy, go and tell her.'

'Aw, Gran-Flan, here we go!'

'What?' The word resounded round the room. 'What did you say?' She now picked up her ear trumpet and, putting it to her ear, she turned her head to the side to enable Eddie to shout into it, 'I said all . . . right . . . Gran . . .!'

The ear trumpet was replaced on the table, the round eyes stared at him. 'Did you?' she said, and he mouthed at her, 'Yes, Gran,' before moving hastily away from her chair.

She was a witch. He didn't know how he'd be able to stand her for three months. And not only her. No, by the looks of things, not only her. There was that Hal Kemp too. He didn't like the man. He hadn't liked him before today but now he liked him less . . .

Fifteen minutes later they were all sitting down in the dining room, which, like the parlour, was solidly and comfortably furnished.

The meal was substantial, consisting of cold meats and pickles and a dish of boiled potatoes from which they all helped themselves. This was followed by large helpings of apple and custard, and it was unfortunate that Eddie wasn't partial to custard.

'Don't you like it?' The bawl almost made him jump in his seat. What it actually did do was to cause him to choke, and he spluttered, 'Aye. Yes, I like it.'

24

'What did you say?'

He turned his face full towards her and spelt out with his lips, 'Yes, I like it.'

When she picked up the trumpet and put it to her ear he closed his eyes for a moment before standing up and, leaning over Penny, yelled into the trumpet, 'Yes, I like it.'

'Don't bawl; I want me head left on me shoulders.'

Oh Lord!

It must have been the look on his face that caused his grandfather to put his foot out under the table and give a couple of taps on his boot, but Eddie, not as yet broken into the ways of under-table complicity, raised his head and smiled at his grandfather. Then realised immediately it had been the wrong thing to do for his grandmother was bawling now, 'What's going on, eh? Signals above and below board. Davy Flannagan, what are you putting the boy up to?'

'Nothing, Maggie, nothing.' Mr Flannagan's voice was quiet but his lips moved widely. 'Not a thing, not a thing. Don't frash yourself.'

'Who's frashing themselves? That'll be the day when I frash meself about any of you. Have you finished?' She turned now to Penny.

'Yes, Gran.' Penny spoke quietly, at the same time nodding her head, and Mrs Flannagan, nodding back towards her, shouted, 'That's a good girl. You don't bawl. Well, if we've all had our fill we'll be like the beggars, we'll go when we're served, eh?' And she startled Eddie afresh by bursting into deep laughter.

Really! She was a character. And how had she

known that his granda was signalling to him? And that laugh, it was bigger than herself, than two of her. Even Mrs Wallis, her who lived along the street and was seventeen stone and gave great belly laughs, she couldn't come up to his granny.

In the sitting room once more, Mrs Flannagan monopolized the conversation. Addressing Penny first, she said, 'You know you're going to a different school, don't you? Your legs won't carry you to that one back in the docks.'

'Yes, Gran.'

'You'll like this school over at Marsden. I saw the mistress. She's a sensible woman.'

Eddie was listening with interest now. He knew that Penny was to go to a school at Marsden, but that his granny had seen the mistress came as a surprise to him. He had the idea that his granny never left the house for she was a dead-old woman, near sixty-six years old.

'And you!'

Eddie blinked. He'd have to get over being startled by her. It wasn't only her voice, it was her quick movements. She might be old but she was springy as a whippet at a rabbit coursing.

'Your granda's mapped out a way for you. It'll shorten your journey to work. Middle dock, isn't it?' She didn't wait for an answer but went on, 'Although in my day I walked four miles to school and thought nothing of it, an' glad to go. 'Twasn't everybody who could go to school in my day, so sleet, hail, or snow I went. But now they make them soft . . . You'll go by the cemetery and come out at the Chichester. He says it'll cut quite a bit off. You did, didn't you?' She was looking at her husband now.

'Yes, yes, I did, Maggie.' Mr Flannagan nodded towards his wife.

Changing the subject abruptly now, she said, 'Your mother should come back a new woman. A wreck she is, a wreck. But what else could you expect, living as she has done for all these years, hand to mouth.'

'She hasn't lived from hand to mouth.' Eddie found that he was bawling now.

'What did you say?' His granny picked up the trumpet and put it to her ear, and he rose from his seat and yelled into it. 'She didn't live from hand to mouth, me da had a good job. He looked after her well and thought the world of her. And she of him. Don't you say anything against me da, I'm tellin' you, 'cos if you do I'll walk out.'

The black circle of the trumpet slowly moved away from his mouth, and in its place was the face of his granny, the brown eyes staring up at him, and his own brown ones almost black now with the intensity of his feelings glared back into them.

And her next words incensed him further because, slowly but not so loud now, she said, 'Your father was a docker. That's what he was when my daughter married him. He hadn't one penny to rub against the other; he hadn't even a place to take her; they were in lodgings for almost six months and there was a time when things were even worse when you were both very small and she starved herself to feed you. Your father was a docker . . .'

27

'He was a gaffer in the docks, he rose to be a gaffer.'

'Gaffer! What's a gaffer?'

He noticed that she had understood that word all right, and she went on, 'Anybody could be a gaffer, anybody who shouted the loudest could be a gaffer.'

'Then you could be one!' As he spoke he pulled the ear trumpet round towards his mouth again and repeated, now yelling into it, 'You could be one then!'

He was standing straight when she took the trumpet from her ear and pressed her hand over the side of her face. His grandfather was on the other side of her now, his voice soothing, saying, 'Maggie. Maggie. Let up, will you. Let up.'

Her hand still pressing her ear, she turned her head to the side and looked at Eddie, and it was in genuine remorse now that he said, 'I'm sorry; I'm sorry, Gran, if I hurt you.'

Whether or not she understood him he didn't know, for what she said now was, 'I'm going to me bed.'

As Mr Flannagan went to help her to her feet she smacked his hand away from her arm, saying, 'Stop your fussing, I'm not senile, not yet, and I think I can find me own way to me bed.' And on this she actually marched from the room, her short thin body as stiff as a soldier's.

'Pay no attention, boy.' Mr Flannagan now pressed Eddie onto the couch; then himself sat down and drawing Penny towards his knee, he patted her hand and said, 'Don't look so worried,

28

child. Your granny doesn't mean half what she says.'

'Our da was a nice man, Granda.' Penny swallowed deeply now.

'I'm sure he was, my dear. In fact I know he was. But you see' – the old man turned his head towards Eddie now – 'women are a different kettle of fish from men. Perhaps you've already found that out. And if they've got a daughter they have ideas for her. And your granny had ideas for your mother. Oh, big ideas. There was a first officer on my ship, he's a captain now, and that's who your granny wanted for your mother, a captain, like I was. And your mother liked him. Yes, she did, because the day she came on to my ship presumably to see me, it was, I know, to have a look at him too. It was on that day, too, a day of unloading, that she slipped on the deck. And who should break her fall but a fine, sturdy looking docker who eventually became your father. Did you know that?'

He looked from one to the other, and they both shook their heads dumbly.

No, Eddie thought, he didn't know that was how his ma had met his da, it was news to him.

'As you said' – Mr Flannagan was looking down on Penny – 'your father was a good man and my girl must have recognized that in him straight away, because when we next docked in the Tyne, it was to find my girl was a married woman and your granny distraught.'

'You see' – he put his head to the side now – 'your mother was her only child and had been her constant companion. But then what power has a mother, or father for that matter, against the power of a young woman in love?'

He looked at them, and they looked back at him. A log fell in the grate and sent sparks up the wide chimney. 'Ah!' He lay back now, smiled at them; then closing his eyes, he said, 'Go and talk to Daisy. She's young company, good company is Daisy.' He opened his eyes. 'Have you seen your rooms?'

'No, not yet, Granda,' Eddie said quietly.

'Then Daisy will show you, and much more besides if I know Daisy. Go on with you.'

Daisy was at the sink and at their entry she turned her head and said, 'Come for your bundles, have you? I'm nearly finished the dishes, then I'll take you up. Did you like your supper?'

'Yes, thank you.' They both spoke together, and Penny added, 'There was a lot of everything.'

'Oh aye, it's a good meat house, the missis never stints. Do you hear that?' She jerked her head towards the square kitchen window that showed black against the night. 'The wind's getting up an' it's blowin' this way, so there could be some pickings on the beach the morrow.'

'What kind of pickings?' Eddie walked slowly towards her, and she looked at him as she dried her hands and answered, 'Oh, it all depends. Sometimes just wood, empty barrels and crates an' such; but then it might be a cask with something in.' She laughed now. 'I once found a cask, just a little one, but it was full of rum. By! the master wasn't half pleased, he gave me a whole half dollar. And once I saw a dead man.'

As Penny put her fingers across her lips and

screwed up her face, Daisy said, 'Oh, you needn't be frightened, dead people can't hurt you, but they look awful. This one was bobbing on the water like a cork. I came scampering back an' told the missis, and she came down with me. Mind, she had a job 'cos I can hardly get down meself. Anyway, down she got, and she pulled him in shore, then sent me to the coastguard station. An' I was glad to go, I can tell you, 'cos he looked awful.'

'Aw, I wouldn't want to go down there.' Penny shuddered, then added, 'I would rather go to Marsden Grotto; I've been to the Grotto.'

'Who hasn't!' Daisy hung the coarse towel up on a nail, straightened her apron and pulled her starched cap down about her ears. 'Everybody goes to the Grotto,' she said. 'It's like August Bank Holiday every week in the summer, people going to the Grotto. But as the missis says they're not real caves, they were cut out of the rock. There're real caves along here though, real deep ones.'

'Where?' The abrupt question brought Daisy round to face Eddie; but seemingly she had no quick answer ready for him for she didn't reply until she had rolled down the sleeves of her blue print dress and buttoned the cuffs, and then she said, 'Well, all along the coast.'

'Have you seen any?'

She slanted her eyes at him. 'No, I haven't; but . . . but the missis says there's caves all along the coast, and if she says there's caves all along the coast' – her voice was now rising – 'then there are caves all along the coast.'

'But have you been in a cave, in a deep one?'

Daisy pressed her lips tightly together and wagged her head. 'No, Mr Smarty, I haven't been in a deep one, but I have in the little ones. An' there's some in our cove.' She pointed again to the window. 'But I believe what the missis says, and Mr Van an' all.'

'Mr Van, who's he?'

'He's a gentleman, a very nice gentleman, kind and nice. He . . . he picks pebbles and stones and things along the beach and cliff tops.'

'Pebbles and stones, what does he pick them for?'

'How should I know?' Her chin shook with impatience. 'He sort of collects them for their colours and things. Min . . . mineral somethings they have inside them. He lodges with Biddy, Biddy McMann, but he's soon goin' home to his family. He's got three little girls and a little boy, an' he tells me about them.'

'Where does he live, this Mr Van? I mean where does he come from?'

'Belgium.'

'*Belgium*!'

'Yes, that's what I said, Belgium, and his name isn't Mr Van, it's Van something, but I can never remember the other part, it's a funny soundin' name. All foreign names are funny soundin'. But I know one thing, when he goes I'll miss the coppers that he gives me on a Sunday for collecting the pebbles and things.'

'You collect pebbles for him?'

'Aye, when I can, like on me half-day.'

'Could we come with you?' Penny asked

32

eagerly now, and Daisy appeared to consider a moment before she answered, 'I don't see why not. But I don't suppose he'll dish out any more coppers.'

'Who's wantin' his coppers?' Eddie's tone was indignant, and Daisy rounded on him now, crying, 'Well, I was only tellin' you. By! you are touchy. Aw, come on' – she stumped away from them down the kitchen – 'I'll show you where you're sleepin'. And mind' – she turned as she neared the door and looked at them both – 'you've got to make your own beds. I'll sweep your rooms out but you've got to empty your slops and do the rest yourselves because I'm run off me feet from mornin' till night when Biddy isn't here.'

'You needn't worry about us, we can clean our own rooms.'

'All right, Mr Clevershanks, I'll keep you to that.'

Penny followed Daisy through the door, but Eddie remained where he was for a moment. Eeh! he felt he wanted to skelp her lug, he did that. She was a cheeky monkey.

When he reached the landing, which was like a wide corridor with doors going off both sides, the weak rays of a small oil lamp hanging from a hook on the wall showed him Penny and Daisy disappearing through a doorway at the far end, and when he, too, entered the room Daisy was lighting a candle and saying, 'It isn't very big but it's comfortable. And I've put the bonny patchwork quilt on it for you' – she now pointed to the bed – 'and a clippie mat down, 'cos when you

33

step on the lino in the morning it freezes you right up to your gullet.'

'Well now, that's you settled.' She smiled at Penny, then turned to Eddie and stared at him for a moment before dipping her knee and, adopting a most servile expression, she said, 'Would you care to come an' see your apartment, sir?'

Eddie, staring down on her, had the desire to burst out laughing at her antics, but that, he warned himself, would never have done. So what he did say was, 'I can see you gettin' your lug skelped one of these days.'

At this Daisy became her usual self again, and giving a huh! of a laugh, she said, 'Well, there's one thing sure, Mr Dockworker' – she now wagged her head at him – 'it won't be you that'll do it.' And turning she went from the room with Penny, who was trying to suppress a giggle, following her.

Again he remained still as the thought came to him that although he was the grandson of her mistress and she herself was only a maid, she treated him as someone of no account, in fact as not even her equal. Well, he would see about this; aye, before he was much older he would see about this.

'Are you comin'?' It was a hissed whisper, and when he took the few steps on to the landing, Daisy pointed to the door next to Penny's bedroom, saying, 'That's Mr Kemp's room, but over there' – she now pointed to a door in the opposite wall – 'that's the master's and missis's room. It's the biggest one in the house an' it looks out

34

on to the front. And you, your lordship, are in the next one.' She tip-toed now across the landing and, pushing open the door, she said, 'Here!' and stood aside to allow Eddie to pass before her.

The room was in pitch darkness and he hissed at her, 'Where's the candle?'

'You're privileged, you don't have a candle, you have a lamp. Stand still a minute an' I'll light it.'

When the room was illuminated, Eddie looked round and was scarcely able to conceal his surprise. It was almost three times the size of Penny's room. There was a single brass bedstead, the head of which stood against a stone wall, the same as could be seen on the outside of the house. It crossed his mind that it would have looked better white-washed. Then his eyes were drawn to the left of him where a huge wooden cupboard seemed to take up the whole of the side wall.

Following his look, Daisy pulled open two doors in the middle of the cupboard, saying, 'It's a wardrobe sort of, but you'd need some clothes to fill it. And over there' – she turned and pointed – 'that's your wash-hand stand. But if you take it into your mind to wash up here you'll have to cart your own water up and down.

'Well, there you are.' Daisy now looked at Eddie but he was staring at the floor flanking the bed and there might have been the merest twinkle in his eye as he said, 'There's something missing.'

'Missin'? What do you mean, missin'?'

'Well, where's the clippie mat? And there's not even lino on the floor, only bare boards.'

'And that's what you're gettin', bare boards, 'cos that'll be the day when I go to the trouble of puttin' a mat down for you and havin' to lug it downstairs and shake it in the yard. Oh aye, that'll be the day.'

As she walked jauntily from the room, Eddie looked at his sister, and when he jerked his chin upwards Penny bit on her lip; then they smiled at each other and Eddie said softly, 'Do you want to go to bed?'

'Aye, Eddie, I'm tired.'

'Me an' all. Good-night then.' He went towards her, then shyly he bent forward and kissed her on the cheek. 'That's from me ma. She said to give it to you and tell you not to worry.'

When she threw her arms impulsively around him and leant against him for a moment, he stood stroking her hair, until he became aware of Daisy standing once again in the doorway; and now he almost pushed Penny from him and when she said, 'Good-night, Eddie,' he answered gruffly, 'Good-night,' and closed the door abruptly on them both.

A few minutes later, having decided that the warmest place would be in bed, he was pulling his shirt over his head when the door opened abruptly and Daisy's face came round it, and she flung her voice across at him in a hoarse whisper, saying, 'Would you like a mug of cocoa? Penny's gona have one. I could bring it up when I bring the missis's.'

He was standing stiffly, his shirt held in front of his bare chest, his face grim, and he had to swallow twice and cough before he could say, 'Aye ... thanks ... ta.'

Her smile was brighter than the lamplight; it seemed to illuminate her face as she bobbed her head at him.

When the door was closed he stood staring at it; then dropping down on to the side of the bed, his head moved slowly from side to side as he said to himself, 'Eeh! what can you make of her?' In a way she was as big an irritant as his granny, only different, sort of.

3

The wind was still high; it tore their voices away.

Looking to where Daisy was running helter-skelter along the sand followed by Penny, Eddie knew it was no good him yelling to stop them going round the point of rock that jutted out from the cliff proper and where the incoming tide was already lapping it, and so he took to his heels and dashed after them. When he came abreast of Penny he didn't stop, but ran until he had overtaken her, grabbed Daisy's shoulder and brought them both tumbling face forward onto the sand.

'What do you think you're up to?' Daisy was rising from her knees puffing and gasping, her hands to her head straightening her round straw hat that was held in place by a band of tape which passed over the top of it and under her chin. 'An' look at me Sunday coat!' She now banged her hands all over the front of the black serge coat that reached to her ankles.

'Couldn't you see the tide coming in?' Eddie shouted as he pointed towards the rocks ahead of them.

'Aye, I'm not blind.'

'You were going to go round there.'

'What! You're up the pole, that's what you are. Me goin' round there! Don't be daft; I'd be up to me neck in water in a few feet, there's a groyne there. I know this stretch. Anyway, what made you think I was goin' round there?'

'Well' – Eddie rose to his feet now and dusted the sand from the knees of his trousers – 'you were running helter-skelter for it. And you an' all.' He turned on Penny.

'I wasn't. I was only running. An' what's the harm in that?' Penny now tossed her head in unusual defiance.

After staring at her for a moment, Eddie let out a long breath and turned from them and retraced his steps along the cove. She was right; what was the harm in that? What was the matter with him? All of a sudden he had been filled with panic as he saw them rushing towards that point of rock.

It was a weird place, this, he didn't like it. He looked at the towering rocks. The whole surface right up to the top looked tormented as if a giant hand had clawed at it. He could understand the ruggedness of the bottom of the cliffs where the tide lashed up to all of five feet above his head and had left its waving signature here and there with lines of seaweed and debris, but that it should be the same right up to the top puzzled him.

He half glanced over his shoulder now to see where the girls were and saw them near the foot of the cliff scattering the pebbles. Reluctantly he turned about and went to join them, telling himself as he did so that it was like looking after two bairns. What he wanted to do was to go for a brisk tramp, not dawdle along here when the wind and the sea deafened you. Last night he had gone to sleep with the sea in his ears and it had woken him up this morning. Why did some boys want to go to sea, and men like his grandfather spend their lives on it? They could keep the sea for him.

He kicked at some loose small rocks, and as they scattered his eyes followed a white object and he bent down and picked it up. It was oval-shaped like a miniature egg, and perfectly smooth all round. Fancy – he shook his head as he turned the stone within his fingers – he had never seen such a pure white stone before.

'Look!' He went quickly towards the girls now holding out his hand. 'Is this the kind of thing you're looking for?'

'Oh, that's bonny an' all white, oh, it is.' Daisy took the stone reverently from his hands. 'Eeh! I've had pieces that were white in parts but I've never seen a smooth one like this. It's a lovely stone. You'll likely be a lucky picker.'

As she handed it back to him, he shook his head, saying, 'I don't want it, you keep it.'

'Honest?'

'Yes. What good is it to me?'

'Oh, ta, thanks.' The bright beam spread over her face again. Mr Van'll like this one. Ta,' she said again.

He turned now and looked towards the water, saying, 'The tide's coming in fast; don't you think we'd better be going up?'

Daisy paused as she was about to bend down again; then as if making a concession because of his gift, she said, 'Aye, I suppose you're right. But it'll be a good half-hour afore it reaches here.'

The three of them moved along the beach now, Daisy and Penny skipping on ahead again, stopping only where the sand gave way to shingle to scan the pebbles, before running on once more. Just like two bairns let out of school, Eddie thought. Somehow, they made him feel old and lonely. He nipped at his lower lip, thrust his hands deep into his pockets and walked with his head down, thinking now, I wonder how she's getting on.

He missed his mother. He'd known he'd feel lonely without her, but hadn't expected to have this lost feeling again. He had felt like this after his father died. Sundays had been a special day for both him and his mother. After he came back from his tramp she always had a big tea ready for him, and after tea they would sit around the fire if it was winter, or they would go walking down to the South Park if the weather was fine. She liked walking in the park.

His thoughts were creating a funny feeling in his chest. It rose into his throat and he had to swallow quickly. He jerked his head upwards as if to throw it off, then paused in his step as he saw in the distance Daisy and Penny talking to a man.

He didn't hurry; his step was slow and it seemed a long time before he reached them. And when he did the man spoke immediately, saying, 'Well! well! so this is your brother.' The voice

41

didn't sound English, although the man himself looked no different from any Englishman, at least a well-to-do one.

'How-do-you-do?'

'I'm all right . . . thank you.'

'Miss Daisy here tells me that you found this.' He held out the white stone. 'Very nice, very nice indeed.'

Eddie didn't look at the stone but he looked at the man. He had a pleasant face, his side whiskers were slightly grey, as was his pointed beard; he was of medium height and thin with it, and altogether he bore out Daisy's description of being a nice man. He was saying in his word-spaced fashion: 'It has been a wild night.'

'Yes, it has.' Eddie thought he should have added, 'sir'. He watched the man now put his hand in his pocket and bring out some loose silver, and when he handed Daisy a sixpence, she exclaimed on a high note, 'Eeh! a tanner! Eeh! I've hardly got any for you. Was it because of the white one?'

'Yes' – he nodded at her – 'we'll say it's because of the white one. And here, young lady.' He bent towards Penny, offering her a sixpence too, but Penny hesitated and looked at Eddie. However, any protest Eddie might have made was cut off by the man saying, 'I cannot give to one without the other, now can I?'

'No, well I suppose not.' Eddie found himself smiling, and when he nodded towards Penny it was to give her permission to take the money.

'Oh, thank you, sir, thank you.'

'You . . . are . . . welcome . . . that is what they

42

say here, don't they? You . . . are . . . welcome.'

They were all laughing together now, and when they turned about and walked along the beach the girls presently went on ahead again and Eddie was left with the man.

'I . . . I understand from Miss Daisy that your mother is ill?'

'Yes, sir.' It seemed easy to say 'sir' to this man.

'I am sorry to hear that. Will she be away long?'

'For three months.'

'Three months! But you will like living with your grandmother.'

Eddie cast his eyes sidewards, and as his gaze met that of the man he felt able to say, 'I don't know so much about that, sir; she's a bit of a tartar.'

'All grandmothers are bits of tartars. I know because I have four children and their grandmother is a . . . bit . . . of . . . a . . . tartar.'

The man laughed, and Eddie laughed with him, at the same time feeling grateful to him, for that awful womanish feeling had gone from his chest.

They had come to a sort of gulley which had eaten its way somewhat into the cliff; but although the sides were still very steep, a way up to the top had been made by a rough series of steps that had been cut out many years before, but which had now been reduced by wind and weather to mere toe grips.

They were all out of breath when at last they reached the top of the cliff; but with Daisy and Penny their breathlessness seemed to last only for a moment, for once again they were scampering away.

As the man stood gasping he looked after them and said, 'What it is to be young. And your sister, she's very pretty. Indeed, yes, she is very pretty.'

Yes, he supposed Penny was pretty. His mother was always on about her being pretty. If you got down to facts it was because of her prettiness that he was landed out here. If she had been a plain Jane nobody would have bothered to look the side she was on, and they could both have been at home now.

'Well, I must be going.'

Eddie turned to the man. 'You're not going back along the cliff top?'

'No. I have an appointment at Marsden.'

'Oh. Good-bye then.'

'Good-bye, young man. Good-bye. It's been very pleasant meeting you.'

His mind was answering, 'And you,' but he couldn't make his tongue use the words. He just jerked his head in acknowledgement of the compliment, or courtesy, or whatever it was, and turned and hurried after the girls. But as he did so he thought, I could go for a tramp, there's still some time till dark.

Well, why didn't he? He was looking at Penny and Daisy racing back towards him, their skirts held up almost to their knees, and instead of his mind giving him a direct answer to his question, it said, 'Eeh! she's a wild young monkey, that Daisy.'

When Daisy came panting up to him and

gasped breathlessly, 'Mr Van went then?' he replied, 'Well, he's not here, so he must have.'

'Oh! smarty. Anyway, he's nice, isn't he?'

'He's all right.'

She stared at him for a moment, then said, 'He didn't give you anything so you can have half of me sixpence because it was your stone, you found it.'

'I don't want half of your sixpence!' He scowled at her now, then marched off towards the house, and she shouted at him, 'You needn't get your shirt out then.'. . . .

They were walking one on each side of him now and Penny, looking across him, said, 'You don't mind going in early on your day off, Daisy?'

'Why no, if I didn't go in I'd just walk about, wouldn't I? It's different when you go into Shields, there's things to see there.'

'Haven't you anybody to go to?' Eddie asked, and Daisy looked at him first before turning her gaze straight ahead again and saying, 'No, nobody. I don't remember me ma, and me da was drowned off the banks.' She pointed over the sea in the direction of the sandbanks. 'I was just on six then, an' I was livin' with Mrs Day. I called her auntie, but she wasn't me auntie. She had seven bairns and it was me job to look after the three youngest.'

'And you just on six!' There was a large blob of doubt in Eddie's tone.

'Aye.' Daisy turned her head abruptly towards him. 'You don't believe me? Well, I can remember pushin' the two young ones down Ocean Road in the push-chair, right to the sands, when I was just on five.'

'Oh, I can believe you, Daisy.' Penny's voice held its usual conciliatory note, as it always did on these occasions when her big brother was getting on the wrong side of someone. 'Janie Tyler, she lives right at the bottom of our street, she's not six yet, and she looks after the two youngest. And she's good at it, she's always cleaning their noses.'

'How did you come to work for me granny?' Eddie's tone was slightly more credulous now.

'Oh that! That was through Biddy McMann.' Daisy laughed now. 'Biddy saw I was being worked to death an' she said I wouldn't be reaching the old age of ten the way I was being treated, so she bluffed, as she can, you know. Oh aye, she can bluff all right. She said she was a distant relation of me da's, and she took me away. I stayed with her in the cottage, and I went to school regular until I was thirteen. Then I was bad for a bit and when the school board didn't trouble me she got me set on with Mrs Flannagan.'

'Why don't you go an' see her on a Sunday then?' Eddie was looking fully at her now.

'For the simple reason that she's never there on a Sunday, she goes across the water to Howdon to see her son.'

'I thought her leg was bad?'

'If she was walkin' on stumps she'd still go across to see him.'

'Why doesn't he come across to see her?'

'Well' – her tone was pert again – 'if you want to know, her son's a cripple. He wasn't born crippled but she says he is now, he's all screwed up with rheumatics and things.'

'Oh!'

46

'Yes, oh! You want to know the far end of the smell of a dead fish, you do.' And on this and a high laugh she sped away again.

This time Penny didn't immediately follow her, but looking at Eddie, she said, 'She's funny, isn't she? Merry like. I like her; don't you, Eddie?'

Eddie considered for a number of seconds before he deigned to reply and then he said, 'Well, not much . . . Oh, I suppose she's all right; but she's too bloomin' cheeky for the size of her.'

'You like her!' Penny's voice was teasing now, and he turned on her, almost growling, 'I don't! Not like that. I'd like to slap her face half the time.'

'You like her!' Penny was rushing backwards now, and when she cried again, 'You like her!' he spurted forward but not so quickly that he could catch her, and when she reached Daisy, Daisy caught her hand and together they ran squealing over the grass, along by the front of the house and into the yard, there to be greeted at the half-open kitchen door by Mrs Flannagan.

'Running like that, like mad March hares on a Sunday! Come in with you!' She pulled open the bottom half of the door, and when, panting, their heads down, they passed her, she turned her steely glance on Eddie, shouting, 'Have you gone back into your childhood? But I suppose it's a change from the big fellow you think yourself to be. Get in there!'

When she placed her hand between his shoulder blades and pushed him further into the kitchen he stiffened, then turned sharply round

47

on her. For a moment they faced each other, the little straight-backed woman in the grey cotton dress with the billowing skirt, and the gangling boy, like two combatants not unfairly matched.

Eddie was the first to give in. His head drooped. He turned away and towards the table where Daisy was standing looking at the set meal and exclaiming, 'Oh! it's a nice tea, Mrs Flannagan.'

'What?'

Daisy now came round the table. She had her straw hat in one hand and with the other she lifted up the trumpet from her mistress's breast, where it was hanging by a black silken cord, and putting it to Mrs Flannagan's ear, she shouted, 'You've set a lovely tea . . . Is the master coming in an' all?'

'Well, where do you think he would eat, in the coal house?'

Daisy laughed heartily at this. Then turning round, she spoke to both Penny and Eddie, saying softly now, 'She often makes the tea when I'm out on a Sunday, always in the sitting room, but she's laid it here the day 'cos there's more of us. Isn't it nice?'

When Penny nodded at Daisy, Mrs Flannagan cried, 'What's she saying?'

Once more Daisy was shouting into the trumpet, 'I said it was nice of you.'

'Don't you try to butter me up, girl.' And the trumpet was pulled from Daisy's hand, and she, her face one bright smile, looked at her mistress and, shaking her head, mouthed widely, 'I'm not. I'm not, missis.'

'Get your things off, then go and tell the master the meal's ready.'

'Aye, missis.'

'Are you two not staying?' Mrs Flannagan was now dividing her gaze between Penny and Eddie. 'Well if you are, get your things off and wash your hands. See your nails are clean; I'll have no funeral fingers at my table, in the kitchen or elsewhere.' And so saying she went bustling about the kitchen.

Meanwhile Eddie, after taking his coat off, went and scrubbed his hands under the pump in the yard. When he returned, his grandfather was already seated at one end of the table and his grandmother at the other. Penny and himself sat down at one side and Daisy opposite them; but there was still a seat vacant, and he saw his grandmother looking towards it. Presently, glancing at her husband, she said, 'Going to bed on a Sunday afternoon, sleeping off his drink! Well, I won't have it. I'll tell him.'

It was at this moment that the door leading from the hall opened and Hal Kemp entered the room, and his voice was cheery as he sat down at the table and said, 'Good. Good; that's what I can do with, a cup of tea and a bite.'

It was evident that Hal Kemp was aware of his aunt's displeasure and so he turned his attention to Daisy saying, 'Been for your Sunday jaunt?'

Daisy now looked towards her mistress. but seeing that her eyes were downcast she dared to answer him, otherwise she would have remained silent because she wasn't allowed to speak at the table. Quickly she muttered, 'Aye; we all went and we got some lovely stones, at least Eddie did, a big white one, and Mr Van gave me and Penny sixpence each.'

'He seems a very enthusiastic stone gatherer, this Mr Van.' It was Mr Flannagan speaking now, and he turned towards Hal Kemp and said, 'I've never happened to meet him, what's he like? What's your opinion of him?'

'Me? Oh!' Hal Kemp moved his head from side to side while screwing up his face and replying, 'Don't know the man, except I've seen him at Biddy's when I've dropped in. No more than good-day passed atween us, otherwise I've no idea.'

Eddie was about to transfer a succulent piece of boiled ham to his mouth but he held it stationary for a second midway between his plate and his chin as his glance rested on Daisy. Daisy was looking at the downcast head of Hal Kemp, and her mouth was open and her eyes stretched wide. Suddenly she blinked, closed her mouth and went on with the meal . . .

It wasn't until later in the evening when the table was cleared and he had been reluctantly brought in to a game of ludo with the girls that he asked Daisy quietly, 'What made you look like that when Hal Kemp said he didn't know your Mr Van?'

Daisy did not look at him, but went on shaking the dice in the wooden container, and when she threw it on the table she said, 'Five,' before adding, 'He was lying, that's why.'

'Lying?'

'Aye, he said he didn't know Mr Van. Well,

I've seen them at least twice, no, three times talking together. Once they were on the beach where we were the day, walking along it.' She now turned and looked full at Eddie and asked quietly, 'Why should he lie about that?'

Eddie made no reply, only shook his head, but he said to himself, Aye, why should he lie about that?

4

Eddie thought no more about Hal Kemp and the fact that he had lied about his acquaintance with the foreigner until nearly four weeks later. The time between had been taken up with his work and the longer trek to and from it, and also his twice-weekly visits to the Institute to further his study of engineering and the homework these entailed. Then there was the weekly letter to his mother. He might receive as many as three from her but he was sure she understood that he couldn't manage more than one because letters took a lot of thinking about. He had told her he was so glad she was feeling better, that Penny was well and happy and was great pals with Daisy, and that he himself was in the best of health, although he got very tired towards nine o'clock at night and couldn't wait to get to bed; and lastly, his granda was well, and his grandma ... well, she was the same as ever. He once finished his letter with a joke, saying, 'If I bawl at you when you come home don't blame me; you will have asked for it by making me stay here.'

He never mentioned Hal Kemp because he had nothing to say about the man except that he didn't like him. That was until one Wednesday evening when he was hurrying back from work.

His grandfather had mapped out the route for him. This shortened considerably the distance between the house and the dock, but even so it was almost dark before he reached the cliff top.

Taking this route, his approach to the house was towards the back garden. He had thought recently that in future he would spend some time on a Sunday clearing a path through the bramble and rough scrub which would lead directly to the yard. There were one or two places where the railings were broken down and he had tried to make his way through from there but hadn't got very far. A straight path would only save a couple of hundred yards or so but even that would be something, he considered, because he always felt dead beat by the time he had skirted the railings and come round to the front of the house, especially if there was a strong wind blowing off the sea, for it aimed to bend him backwards as it had done all the tangled greenery.

But tonight he had just turned the bottom corner of the railings when he stopped and screwed up his eyes. The light was fading fast. Moreover, there was a high wind blowing and he thought for a moment he was imagining that the errant tangle of branches hanging over the railings had taken on the form of a man. Then, his vision clearing, he recognized that it *was* a man, it was Mr Van. But what was he doing? He was looking up over the garden towards the back of the house and he was whistling. The sound came to him on the wind. It was like a seagull's cry, and yet it wasn't; it was high pitched and the note was long.

When the note stopped, the man continued to look upwards; then placing his hands over his mouth, he again made the strange sound, but louder this time.

It was at this moment that Eddie remembered Daisy saying that Hal Kemp was lying, and he had no doubt in his mind that it was to Hal Kemp the man was calling.

Slowly now Eddie looked towards where a few feet in front of him, the railings were sagging, almost providing a gap into the undergrowth beyond, and so, pressing back against them, he stepped tentatively over them and lowered himself down into the tangle of dead grass, weeds and scrub.

He couldn't see the man now but he would be able to hear if his Uncle Hal, as Penny dutifully called him, came out to meet him.

Seconds take on the time of minutes when you're waiting, and he felt he must have been waiting for at least fifteen minutes before he heard the steps coming through the undergrowth, and on the sound panic seized him. What if Hal Kemp found him here! He'd likely knock him cold. He crouched down until he was leaning on his elbows and the undergrowth formed a black canopy about him, and as he strained his ears it came to him that Hal Kemp must already have made a path from somewhere in the garden – its entrance likely well covered – to the outer railings.

Time passed. He could hear nothing above the

sound of the wind and he was about to rise upwards when the thud, thud of approaching footsteps brought him flat on the ground again; and the sudden drop almost caused him to yell out as a bramble pierced the palm of his hand.

'I can't wait much longer, they're getting impatient.'

That was Mr Van's voice speaking his stilted English.

And now Hal Kemp answering him: 'It's too risky, I'm telling you. I could get years. Anyway, some of these blokes around here would lynch me themselves.'

'Nonsense! It's being carried out all the time. And if anyone has been caught there's those in high places who get them off. It's for their benefit, isn't it?' The man's laughter came to Eddie; and then the voice faded away, saying, 'Anyway, you're being well paid. And there's more . . .'

Eddie remained still. His eyes, stretched wide, gazed into the dark jumble of undergrowth. Hal Kemp was being well paid and by that Mr Van, but for what? And he had thought the man was nice, a gentleman. He was up to something. Smuggling?

Well, it went on, although the coastguards were pretty hot along this stretch. But what were they smuggling, something coming in or something going out? And something big. What had Hal Kemp said? He could be lynched for it by the men around here.

Again he was about to rise to his knees when he was brought stiff and taut by the sound of crushing undergrowth. Hal Kemp must have passed by and he hadn't heard him. He began to sweat. What if he had stood up and come face to face with him? He'd better give him five minutes start to get into the house.

But what was he up to? What? Should he tell his grandfather? No, no. His grandfather was an old man, it might worry him. Yet his grandfather knew that Kemp did a bit of smuggling on the side, or at least receiving, because didn't he tell him to take some stuff to Biddy McMann? And wasn't there always piles of butter and cheese and bacon and such in the house? It didn't come by the grocery cart 'cos he'd seen the order that his granny left on the table. It had included a pound of bacon and a pound of butter, and the way they all ate, a pound of bacon and a pound of butter wouldn't have filled their holey teeth.

He emerged from the undergrowth, dusted himself down, then walked slowly along by the fence, round towards the front of the house and up the yard. And when he opened the kitchen door it was to see Hal Kemp standing in his usual pose with his back to the fire warming his buttocks, and the man yelled, 'Make way for the workman! Let the master of the house sit down and have his meal. Putting us to shame he is. The only one who earns his bread.'

'Shut up!' As Eddie spoke he tossed his cap behind him on to a chair; then almost tearing off his coat while still keeping his eyes on Hal Kemp, he added, 'And there's something in what you say, for I can't see you breakin' your neck with what you do.'

'You cheeky young swine!' Hal Kemp was

advancing slowly round the table towards him now, and Daisy was yelling, 'Eeh! stop it! stop it, both of you!' when the door opened and Mrs Flannagan entered and, taking in the situation straightaway, she cried, 'What's this? Now what's this?'

Quickly Hal Kemp went towards her, but as he was about to pick up the trumpet from her breast she slapped his hand away and, putting the horn to her ear, she said, 'Well, go on.'

'I just made a joke, Auntie, and he turned on me. Bawled his head off, told me to shut up, and that I wasn't pullin' me weight here. Well, you tell him if I'm pullin' me weight or not.' He now nodded furiously towards Eddie as his hands, gripping his belt that slotted through loops in his trousers, tugged savagely at the buckle and tightened it by one further loop before he swung round and left the room.

Mrs Flannagan stared at Eddie. 'You cheeked him?'

'I gave him back as much as he gave me.'

'She can't hear you, man.'

He didn't look towards Daisy where she was gesticulating behind Mrs Flannagan's back, but with an impatient movement of his head he went to his granny's side and yelled into the horn, 'I gave him as much as he gave me. He's always skitting me.' And only just in time did he stop himself from banging the horn down onto her chest.

'You'll get more than a skit before you're finished, young man.'

Not for the first time during the last few weeks did Mrs Flannagan again jump when her grandson

grabbed her ear trumpet; and her face screwed up
as his words resounded through her head: 'Well,
it won't be from the likes of him. He's no good . . .
I'm telling you he's no good. If you only knew.'
He turned abruptly away from her now – he'd let
his tongue run off with him – but when his arm
was gripped and he was pulled round towards her
again and she said, 'What should I know?' he
turned his head to the side and said, 'Nowt.' Then
facing her, he mouthed the word, 'Nowt.' And
again, 'Nowt.'

She let go of his arm but continued to stare at
him. Then she turned her head slowly and looked
towards the kitchen door, which Hal Kemp had
banged closed in his departure, and what she said
now, and in a moderate tone, was, 'Get your wash
and have your meal because you've got to be off
again, haven't you? You're hardly in before
you're out. If you'd had any sense you would
have gone to your home to wash, then gone on to
the Institute from there.'

He gaped at her, his mouth wide. The times he
had wanted to do just that. But he'd thought it
would get her back up and so he hadn't proposed
it. Eeh! she was a marler. All women were mar-
lers . . . except his mother. He was tired and
bored and fed up to the back teeth.

During the time it took him to have his wash
and change his clothes he made up his mind that
he was going to confide the business of Hal Kemp
and that Mr Van to his grandfather, but on enter-
ing the dining room he saw that his grandfather's
chair was empty. Presently when he still hadn't
put in an appearance at the meal he said in an

aside to Penny, 'Where's me granda?' and she, her head down, whispered back, 'He's got a cold, he's in bed.'

Hal Kemp's seat too was empty; and he was glad of that for he doubted if he would have eaten anything if he'd been sitting opposite to him tonight.

It was a comparatively quiet meal, and it wasn't until the end of it that his grandmother spoke; and then she said, 'If you can spare a minute of your valuable time you could look in on your grandfather, he's in bed; but, of course, if you're too busy . . .'

Eddie closed his eyes for a moment, then stared at her, his lips pressed tight together, and on this she cried in her usual voice, 'I know what you're thinking, but you'd better not say it if you don't want my hand across your ear.'

Oh Lord! let him get out. Two more months of this, he'd go barmy, do-lally-tap, up the pole, round the bend and back, the lot.

Five minutes later he was standing by his grandfather's bed. 'How are you, granda?'

'Oh, I'm all right, lad. Just a bit wheezy in the chest, but she's stuck me in here. Wants something to do to pass her time away, you know.' He lifted his head from the pillow now and grinned at Eddie. 'She can't get the better of me when I'm standing on me legs, but I'm helpless when I'm in bed.' He punched Eddie gently in the ribs, then said, 'You off to your classes, lad?'

'Yes, Granda.'

The old man stared at him for a moment, then said, 'What's the matter, you're looking a bit grim? Had a heavy day?'

This was the time he could have said, 'Aye, Granda, but it's not the work that's worrying me, it's that fellow, Hal Kemp.' But his granda wasn't well. What was more he had to be on his way; he wanted to get to the class in time. Even now he doubted if he'd make it, yet he had the desire to linger and not only to talk to his grandfather but to take in this room.

This was the first time he had been in his grandparents' room. Daisy had told him that her mistress was very fussy about her bedroom, to the extent that she cleaned it herself and she didn't like people trotting in and out. He glanced round it now in the light of the lamp. It wasn't all that big and there was a resemblance to his own room next door in that the wall behind the bed was made up of stone blocks. And to the right of him was a cupboard similar to the one in his bedroom; this, too, took up nearly all the side wall. For the rest it was comfortably furnished with a thick carpet on the floor and an easy chair to each side of the bed, besides a big polished dressing table and wash-hand stand.

'What's wrong, lad? Are you missing your mother?'

Realising he hadn't answered his grandfather's previous question, he said, 'Yes. No. Well, it's been a heavy day and . . . Aye I do miss her, Granda.'

'I can understand that, lad, 'cos she was always good company, even as a wee bairn, cheerful and sympathetic like, and she's grown more so with the years. But don't worry, she'll soon be back and then you'll be home again and it will be our turn to be lonely.' He again poked his head forward from the pillow. 'And we will, you know; your granny will miss you.'

'What!' The tone of the one word expressed his disbelief, and it caused his grandfather to wag his finger at him, while saying, 'Now, now! You don't understand your granny. But perhaps you will some day.'

They looked at each other quietly for a moment before the old man said, 'Go on, get yourself away. And take care, for the wind's high. You hear it?' He nodded towards the window. 'It's having a fight with the tide down there.'

Eddie paused in turning from the bed and listened for a moment. Yes, it was as his granda said, the wind was having a fight with the tide, for every now and again it was as if the very sea was coming roaring under the house.

Over the past few weeks he had become used to the sound and it didn't irritate him so much now. At first he had likened it to his grandma's voice. He wished he had got as used to her voice as he had to the sound of the sea. Aw well!

'I hope you'll be better the morrow, Granda.'

'Oh, I'll be up on my pins the morrow. Good-night, Eddie.'

'Good-night, Granda.'

In the kitchen he quickly pulled on his coat, and as he did so Daisy came to his side and whispered, 'I'd look out if I were you; Mr Hal's got it in for you.'

'Don't you worry about me. I can take care of meself.'

'I don't know so much.'

'What do you mean, you don't know so much? Just let him go for me and he'll get more than he's bargained for. I haven't worked in the docks for the past eighteen months running up and down the sides of ships and swinging up hot rivets for nothing. I can hold me own.'

'Daisy isn't meaning that, Eddie.' Penny was standing looking at him now. 'She thinks there's something fishy about him and she's only telling you for your own good.'

He looked from one to the other, then leaning towards Daisy, he said, 'Now I'll tell you something. There's six and two three's atween your wonderful Mr Van and him.'

'What do you mean? Mr Van's a nice gentleman.'

'I don't know so much. You remember what you said to me some time ago about Hal Kemp being a liar and saying he didn't know that Mr Van?'

'Ah-ha.'

'Well, he not only knows him but I think they're as thick as two thieves.'

'What makes you say that?'

'Oh, just something that I heard. An' if I was you I'd be careful of your stone-gathering gentleman.'

'Aw, I'd never mistrust Mr Van. I can tell a good 'un from a bad 'un, and he's a nice man. Why, he even said he could get me a place in Belgium as a nursemaid if I wanted to change.'

'*He what*!'

'You heard. He said if I wanted to change me situation he could get me a place in Belgium as a nursemaid, perhaps to his own children.'

Eddie's mouth was open but his eyes were reduced almost to slits as he peered at her in silence now. Strange thoughts were galloping through his head, fantastic thoughts, thoughts that made him afraid. They were mixed up with snatches of conversation he had overheard among his workmates during such times as they sat having their bait, when they would push each other, and one, Billy Rainer, nearly always choked himself with laughter, so much so that he would roll on the ground.

He heard his own voice asking as if from a distance, 'What did you say to him?'

'Oh, I said, thank you very much and that I might go over to his country one day for a trip when I stopped being afraid of the sea. I told him I'd only once been out in a boat an' I was so sick I wanted to die.' She paused here and thought for a moment, then said, 'He told me that I could go on a big boat and it wouldn't rock much, one bigger than the ferry.'

'Daisy!' He had her by the shoulders now and was actually shaking her. 'You listen to me, now you take no notice of what he says, do you hear? An' don't speak to him again.'

'Ger-away!' She shrugged herself from his hands. 'I *will* speak to him again. He's been very kind to me and he's always very nice an' if him and Mr Hal've got their heads together it's likely only over a bit of smugglin'. Butter, or baccy or some such, what everybody does. An' I bet it was Mr Hal who talked him into it 'cos he could persuade a donkey to sell its hind legs, when he gets going.'

63

Eddie stood considering her words. Very likely she was right. But then, on the other hand, recalling the snatch of conversation he had heard earlier, it appeared to him that Mr Van was in charge of whatever situation they were planning and not Hal Kemp. And what could a man smuggle that he could be lynched for? He was worried ... But look at the time! Anyway, she wouldn't be out till Sunday and afore that his granda would be about again and he would talk the matter over with him.

He turned abruptly from them and, going to the side table, he lit one of the lanterns that was standing on it; then casting a last look back on Penny, he said, 'Get yourself to bed soon.' And she answered dutifully, 'Yes, Eddie.'

That night Eddie didn't sleep well. He was very aware of the sea pounding against the rocks; the wind had gone down but at times it seemed that the very waves were lashing themselves against the walls of the house. And when he did fall asleep he had a very disturbing dream like a nightmare, because he imagined somebody was in the room standing by the side of the bed. It was a man and he was bending over him trying to tell him something, but he couldn't hear what he was saying for the roar of the wind. Then, as in most dreams, everything went topsy-turvy and he thought, Of course I can't hear him because I'm not shouting into her trumpet. Then the man took off his peaked cap and hit him across the face with it. It wasn't a hard blow, more as if he were trying to wake him up.

And he did wake up and with a start and he knew a feeling of fear because he imagined the man was still in the room.

Telling himself to sit up, he shook the sleep from his eyes, and as he did so he could see the outline of the furniture in the room for seconds at a time as the scudding clouds passed over the moon. But there was nothing else there, no one else there. He lay down again, but it was some little time before he got to sleep.

It was Saturday before he could talk to his grandfather. He had finished work at twelve o'clock with the intention of hurrying home and changing, then taking Penny down to the market, and later calling in at the house to see that everything was all right, at the same time having a word with Mrs Angus upstairs, who was keeping an eye on things while his mother was away. But his grandfather hailed him from the stable as he was going towards the kitchen and he turned quickly and said, 'Oh, Granda! it's nice to see you up and about again.'

'Yes, I'm about again, lad; but it isn't without a fight.' His grandfather grinned at him. 'I tell her . . . your granny, she's lost for someone to nurse.' Then his face becoming serious, he added, 'It's as well I'm about again I think because Barney here's' – he pointed back to where the horse stood, its head drooping – 'looking the worse for wear. I'll have something to say to Hal when he comes in. The poor old fellow looks as if he's been worked to a standstill, as if he'd been at it all night. I know Hal's got a living to make, and I'm glad he's taking it seriously, but there's limits to what even a horse can stand.' He walked towards the horse now, saying, 'Did you see any sign of your Uncle Hal on your travels?'

'No, Granda ... Granda.' Eddie was now standing at the head of the horse gently rubbing its muzzle, and his grandfather said, 'Yes; what is it, lad?'

'I think there's something you should know.'

'Well, if you think that, you'd better tell me what it is.'

'It's about Hal Kemp.'

'About Hal? What about him?'

'Well, in the first place he wasn't supposed to know that Mr Van who collects the stones. Well, he did know him, he's known him all along. Daisy pointed this out to me first of all, and then, well, on Wednesday night gone I was on me way home when I saw the man, Mr Van, at the back of the garden there' – he pointed – 'and he was making a funny whistling sound and looking up to the house.'

He paused here, and his grandfather, his misty blue eyes tight on him, said quietly, 'Yes; go on.'

'Well, I thought it was funny and I got down behind the railings and into the scrub, and then I heard somebody coming from the house, and it was Hal Kemp, and when they both passed me I heard a bit of what was said. I couldn't make sense of it, I still can't, but it was this, the man was pressing Hal Kemp to do something and he, I mean Kemp, he didn't seem to like the idea. He said he could get years for doing it, or the men around here would lynch him. And that Mr Van said if he was caught, blokes in high places would get him off, or something to that effect; and that anyway he was being well paid. Can you make out what it means, Granda?'

His grandfather stood staring at him for a full minute before he said grimly, 'No, I can't, lad; but I'm going to make it me business to find out because men around here wouldn't talk of lynching anybody for ordinary smuggling. You're sure that's what they said?'

'Yes, that's what they said, Granda. Aye, I'm sure. Honest to God. And it's been on me mind, worrying me.'

'They didn't mention a commodity, well, like food or spirits, butter, cheese, rum or whisky . . . or, or silks?'

'No Granda. Somehow they didn't seem to be talking about anything like that. Well, you know yourself that goes on from time to time.'

'Yes, yes, I know that, lad. And it's usually Ted Reade's boat they use; and Jimmy Vincent and Jack Biddley are the runners, but they're honest men. Well' – he jerked his head – 'you know what I mean, beating the Customs at the game is dangerous, mind you; oh aye, dangerous, but nevertheless, it's a game and they play it clean, according to their own standards.'

Eddie watched his grandfather walk the length of the stable, his head turned to the side, his teeth nipping his lower lip. Then turning about, he tugged at his bushy beard as he said, 'It could be stones.'

'Stones? Those things he picks . . .'

'No, no, lad, not those kind of stones, precious

stones, diamonds, rubies, stolen stuff from either across the water or over here. And they're clever, those boys who deal with that kind of merchandise. That Mr Van, he collects stones, doesn't he? Oh yes, we know he collects stones. That's a good cover that is. They've got ways of piercing a stone, the pebble ones I mean, and inserting the precious ones into them and covering them up in such a way that it would take a clever man even with his magnifying glass to detect where the splits are. Yes' – he came towards Eddie – 'it could be stones. But' – he paused and shook his head – 'no man would talk of being lynched for carrying stones. No, there's only two things a decent man in Shields would consider lynching another for. Aye, only two things. And I'm going to find out which of them it is, and either one he'll get his marching orders, that's if I don't try to lynch him meself afore that. Truth to tell now, I've never liked the fellow. No, I haven't.' He shook his head vigorously now. 'But he's your granny's nephew and we give him hospitality because of it. But over the year he's been here the tales he's told of his twenty years journeying abroad have contradicted each other. It takes a liar to have a good memory, boy. Yes, it does that, and he's a liar. Well, I'll go and find out what he's up to, an' I'll put the fear of God into him if nothing else . . . I think I know where to find him. There's one man down there who mans a boat and doesn't keep to any standards.'

Of a sudden his grandfather seemed to lose his years and become a vital straight-backed strident captain again, for he now walked briskly towards the door of the stable, saying, 'Come along and have your meal; but say nothing to your granny about this, mind.' . . .

It was half an hour later. The meal was over and Eddie was watching his grandmother remonstrate with his grandfather.

'What do you want to go tramping down there for? The wind's fit to cut you in two, you'll get your death, and you just out of bed.'

He saw his grandfather smile at her, pick up the trumpet and say, 'Whisht! woman.'

'Whisht yourself! If you want to see Peter Morgan I can send for him and he can come up and have a meal the morrow.'

Again his grandfather was shouting into the trumpet: 'Nobody sends for Captain Peter Morgan, you should know that by now, Maggie. And there's the Annual Dinner to arrange.'

'Dinner!' His granny almost spat the word out. 'And Peter Morgan, his head's too big for his hat, always has been. And don't you come back coughing here because you'll look after yourself, 'cos I won't.'

'I'll do that, Maggie.' He was mouthing the words at her now and he clapped his hand against his chest. 'I'll rub meself with candle grease.' There was a splutter to the side of him, and he turned and winked at Daisy who was standing near the hall door. But the gesture wasn't lost on Mrs Flannagan and she rounded on Daisy, yelling, 'Get yourself about your work, girl, or you'll find my hand across your ears.'

'You're in a nice tear the day, aren't you?' His grandfather's voice was soft now as once again he spoke into his grandmother's trumpet, and her voice, too, was strangely soft as she answered, 'Why must you go out? You're asking for trouble.'

'I'm all right.' He patted her shoulder, and when she reached up and buttoned the top button of his thick blue reefer coat, he smiled tenderly down on her, then patted her cheek with his fingers before turning from her and going out of the front door.

As his granny stood at the door watching his grandfather walk smartly across the green sward to where the path led from the yard, the wind blew into the hall, and so strong was it, it raised the rope mats from off the stone flags.

When she finally closed the door and, turning towards Eddie, exclaimed, 'Madness! Madness!' he felt a tinge of guilt. If he hadn't told his grandfather about Hal Kemp likely he wouldn't have gone into the town today.

'And you're going out an' all?'

'Yes, Grandma.' He nodded at her.

'Well, go and get ready. And see that the child is wrapped up against the wind. And get yourself back here afore dark.'

He noticed that she didn't say, 'And you wrap up against the wind too.' She wouldn't care if he froze to death.

'Well, what are you standing there for, your mouth open like a fish? If you're going, go.'

Ooooh! Let nobody say he hadn't tried to like his granny. But I ask you, he appealed to himself, did she ever give him a kind word? Was she ever civil to him? Oh, the sooner he and she parted company the better for all concerned. What a change it would be to talk to a woman who would be civil to you.

When he got back later on this afternoon he'd make out a list of the days he'd have to stay in this house and he'd mark them off one by one, and when he came to the last one he'd spit in her eye. Well, not really. But he would say something to her that would be the equivalent, because if he disliked anybody on this earth it was his granny.

5

'Where is he? Where has he got to?' Mrs Flannagan stopped walking the kitchen floor and sat down heavily on a chair. She looked from one to the other of the three faces staring at her, and it was to Daisy she appealed, saying, 'You know, don't you, Daisy, that he's never been out this late, one o'clock in the morning?'

Daisy, lifting the trumpet gently in her hand, put it to her mistress's ear and shouted, 'Could he have had a drop too much, missis, and be stayin' with that captain?'

Mrs Flannagan shook her head slowly and her voice was unusually quiet as she replied, 'I've never known the drink strong enough that could knock David Flannagan off his legs. But I'll tell you this much, I've had a queer feeling on me all day, I felt he shouldn't have gone. One reason or another I felt he shouldn't have gone. There's something fishy. I don't know what it is, I can't put me finger on it, but it's many years since I've had a feeling like this on me . . . And where's Hal I'd like to know.' Her voice rose. 'He's never here when he's wanted. By! I'll give him a mouthful when he does come in; not hilt nor hair of him have I seen since Friday dinner-time.'

It was Daisy again who took up the trumpet, and now she said, 'He could have gone out with the boats; he does, you know, fishing at the week-ends.'

'Fishing!' Mrs Flannagan drew in a deep breath and her hands gripping the trumpet, she tugged at it for a moment as if she were going to wrench it from the cord around her neck. Then, her hands becoming still, she looked down at them for a moment before lifting her eyes and staring at Eddie, and her voice quiet sounding now, she said, 'I know you've offered twice to go and look for him, but there was a time he would have murdered me if I'd sent anyone in search of him, because that would have meant he wasn't capable of finding his way home, and' – she spread one hand wide – 'there's never been a time when he couldn't carry himself and his drink to the front door, but I'm . . . I'm worried.' When she stopped and stared at him, he said, 'I'll . . . I'll go now, Grandma.'

'Wait!' She put up her hand. 'It isn't likely you'll find him lying on the road because somebody would be bound to come along that way, as far as Biddy's cottage at least, so what you must do is to go first of all and knock up Captain Morgan. He'll likely curse you to hell's flames but tell him I sent you, and ask him, politely like, if Captain Flannagan is still with him.'

'But where does he live, Gran?' As he spoke he picked up the trumpet and repeated in a shout,'Where does he live, Gran?'

'The top of Ogle Terrace, you know that way.

73

You go past the Regimental Drill Hall, then on . . .'

'Yes, yes, I know.' Again he was holding the trumpet to her ear. 'What's the number of the house?'

'No number. He called it after his ship, *The Sea Bream*.'

'Oh aye, I know it.' He nodded at her.

'Away you go then. Wrap up well. And hurry back, boy, will you? Hurry back.' . . .

A few minutes later he was going at a jog trot skirting the garden, then over the rough ground until it levelled out and houses began to loom up in the light of his swaying lantern, one here and there, then a couple together, then streets of them.

He was out of breath when he reached the terrace and as he slowed to a walk he heard a clock somewhere in the town chiming the half hour.

There was a ship's bell hanging to the side of the front door of the house and when he rang it the sound reverberated down the street, and he looked about him apprehensively, thinking it would wake the neighbourhood.

It certainly woke Captain Morgan, for there was the sound of a window being opened. Eddie looked upwards, and it was to hear a voice that outdid his grandmother's.

'Who in blazes is that at this hour?'

'It's me, Captain Morgan.' His face was straining upwards, his voice a hoarse whisper. 'I'm . . . I'm Captain Flannagan's grandson. Me granny has sent me to see if he's here.'

'Who? What? Speak up!'

'I've been sent to find out if me granda's here.'

'Your granda?'

'Yes, Captain Flannagan.'

'Davy Flannagan here? No, boy, he isn't here. Why should he be?'

'He . . . he told me granny he was going to call on you.'

'Well, you go back and tell her that I've never seen Davy for close on two weeks now.'

'Yes, sir.'

'Likely gone out fishin'.'

'Yes, sir.'

He remained looking up until the window was banged closed, then he turned and walked down the narrow path and through the iron gate into the street. The fear that had been on him all night was now turning him sick. He had clamped it down by telling himself that after his grandfather had seen Hal Kemp he had done what he had said he was going to do, visited Captain Morgan. Now he knew he had been deluding himself. But in order to curb his fear from running riot he tried another tack of self delusion when he said to himself: Ted Reade and Jimmy Vincent, what if his granda had gone to see them and then had gone on a night trip with them? . . . But his granny said that he always came back home. Yet women liked to think men were obedient all the time. There could have been occasions when he had stayed out all night and she didn't want to remember them.

He knew where Ted Reade lived; it was in one of the little houses going off the waterfront. Should he go? For answer, he set off at a run now.

Cutting across Fowler Street, he eventually emerged at the top of the Market Square, then went down by the Mill Dam bank and on to the riverfront.

He had passed a number of people on his way and some of them had stopped and looked after him, but no one had as yet tried to check his running, until he felt his arm caught in a vice-like grip and he was brought to a standstill opposite a passage way. In a flash he realized that he was handicapped; if he put up a fight and struck out he'd have to drop the lantern from his right hand; the only other alternative was to use his feet. And he was on the point of doing just this when a voice said, 'Now, young . . . fella-me-lad, where may I ask are you runnin' to? Or who you runnin' from?'

Eddie breathed a deep sigh of relief as he looked up at the constable, and he almost stuttered now, 'I'm-I'm-gona-message. I'm makin' for . . . for Ted Reade's house.'

'Oh! Mr Ted Reade, is it?'

Oh lord! Eddie closed his eyes for a moment. Although Ted Reade had never been caught red-handed, it was well known on the waterfront that he did a bit of business on the side and that he was suspected by the police. In fact, he'd heard of bets being laid on how long he'd last without being caught.

'I'm . . . I'm lookin' for me granda.'

'At Ted Reade's?' There was a deep question in the name.

'Aye, yes . . . Well, it's like this . . .'

'Yes, go on. It's like this, you were sayin'.'

'Well, me granda is Captain Flannagan from Rock End. He didn't come home last night an' me granny's worried.' He now added, 'He's been in bed for days with a cold.'

'Oh, Captain Flannagan.' The pressure on Eddie's arm was slightly released. 'Well, if I know anything about sea captains, and Captain Flannagan in particular, he'll be with his cronies playing cards and likely knocking it back.'

'I . . . I've been to his friend, Captain Morgan, and he hasn't seen him.'

'And Mr Ted Reade' – the constable stressed the mister – 'is he a friend of your grandfather's?'

He had to be careful here, so he said, 'I . . . I don't think so, not a close friend, but he knows him. Mr Kemp, that's me grandma's nephew, he goes out fishing in Mr Reade's boat and others, and he hasn't come back the night either so I just wondered if, well' – his voice trailed away as he ended – 'if they'd all gone together.'

'Come on!'

The constable now walked slowly away along the water-front, then turned up a side street, before stopping at the third house and saying, 'Well, go on, you'd better knock him up, hadn't you?'

Eddie paused for a moment before knocking on the door. There was no answer and he was about to knock again when the constable, leaning forward, gave three thumps on the panel with his doubled up fist.

There now came the sounds of commotion from inside the house and within a few seconds the door was opened to show Mr Reade standing in long woollen linings and a short sleeved woollen vest. He was a medium sized man with broad shoulders, a clean shaven squarish face, and a shock of grizzled brown and grey hair. He looked first at the policeman then at Eddie, then back at the policeman and said, 'Aye, and what's this, may I ask?'

'Aye, you may, Ted, you may. Well, it's like this. This young fellow here is lookin' for his granda – so he tells me – an' he wonders if you've got him inside.'

Eddie cast an apprehensive glance between the policeman and Mr Reade. It was evident that they were well known to each other and that the policeman seemed to be enjoying himself.

'What the hell's this! What you up to?' Mr Reade was nodding towards the policeman now. 'Lookin' for his granda! I've never set eyes on the youngster in me life afore.'

'Well, he seems to know you, Ted, he was makin' straight for your house, so he tells me.'

'Who are you, anyway?' As he spoke Mr Reade stepped back into the passage and, lifting a coat from a peg on the wall, he slipped his arms into it as he muttered, 'Comin' here this time of the night . . . what's your name?'

'Me name's Eddie Morley and me granda's Captain Flannagan from Rock End.'

Now Mr Reade's eyes were stretched wide. 'Captain Flannagan? Well, I know Captain Flannagan, but what do you think he'd be doin' in my house at this time of night? Nobody visits anybody in the middle of the night unless they're up to something, and me, I'm a law abidin' citizen.' He now raised his head and nodded it emphatically towards the policeman.

'Well, I just thought ... I've been to Captain Morgan's and he wasn't there, an' I wondered if you'd seen him about.'

'Seen him? Of course, I've seen him about, I see him about most days because where there's boats you'll see the captain. But thinkin' on't, I haven't clapped eyes on him for the past few days.'

'He's been in bed with a cold, but ... but he came down yesterday to see ... well, he said he was goin' to see Captain Morgan about making arrangements for the annual dinner but as I said he mustn't have gone there ... Me granny's worried.'

'Well, lad, I can't help you. An' I'm still puzzled to know why you made for here at this hour.'

'Well, I thought if your boat was out ... well, he could have taken a trip with you, he goes out fishin' at times.'

'Well, he doesn't go out fishin' with me, lad.' Again Mr Reade jerked his head towards the policeman.

'You know what I think?'

Eddie turned and looked at the constable now. 'I think when you get back you'll find your granda in bed all tucked up and snorin'. It's happenin' all the time. Women get worried about their men and send their bairns scurrying into every pub from the docks to the pier head. Well, young fellow, I think you'd better turn yourself around and make for home, eh?

'We're sorry to have troubled you, *Mr* Reade.'

Again the constable stressed the mister, and Ted Reade answered, 'Aye, I bet you are.'

'Good-night. You can go back to bed now.'

As Eddie muttered his thanks to Mr Reade, the constable turned away and he seemed to be laughing.

And as Mr Reade's door closed with a thunderous bang, Eddie saw that he was indeed laughing.

On the waterfront again, the constable stopped and, looking at Eddie, said seriously now, 'Get back home, lad; and if your granda is there he'll not thank you for all the nuration that's been made about him. But on the other hand' – he paused now – 'if he hasn't got home then the best thing your granny can do is to report the matter to the police station.'

'Yes, aye, all right. Thank you . . . Good-night.'

'Good-night.'

On the return journey home he didn't run, nor did he take the short cut, but he followed the road along the cliff top, and as he walked he swung his lantern from side to side, for who knew, he told himself, but that his granda had got a load on and had dropped down by the wayside and fallen asleep.

He was still swinging the lantern when he entered the yard.

When he opened the kitchen door his granny turned from the chair by the fire and got to her feet, and as she stared at him he shook his head.

When she turned away and slowly sat down again, he went to her side, and, lifting up the trumpet, he spoke quietly into it. 'He didn't go to Captain Morgan's, Grandma.'

The trumpet was wrenched from his hand. 'What?'

He shook his head and mouthed, 'He didn't go there.'

'Then where?'

Again he was speaking into the trumpet. 'I don't know. But . . . but I went to Mr Reade's, who has the boat. I thought he might have seen him or taken him out on a fishing trip, but he hadn't seen him either.'

She took the trumpet from his hand and let it hang slackly between her breasts; then slowly she said, 'Never has he stayed a night away from home unless he was at sea; something has happened to him.'

'No! no! Grandma.' He shook his head. 'He could be playing cards.' Again the trumpet was at her ear. 'I saw a constable and he said that when the captains got together, well, they had a sup over much and they played cards all night.'

She took the trumpet slowly from his hand and she held it in both hers as she said, 'He didn't play cards, he didn't like cards.'

They stared at each other for some seconds before she said, 'You must be very tired, go on to bed.'

'No, no, I wouldn't sleep. I'll lie on there' – he pointed to the settle – 'until it's dawn and then I'll go out and look again. You . . . you go on to bed.' He hadn't spoken into the trumpet but she seemed to understand what he had said, for now she answered, 'I couldn't sleep. But if anything has happened to your granda, that's all I'll ever want to do, go to sleep, go into the long sleep.'

When she turned her head from him he went to the settle and, sitting down, took off his boots; and as he went to lie down he wondered if he should tell her about his grandfather going to see Hal Kemp. But he resisted the urge because, he admitted to himself, he was afraid of her reactions – he could hear her bawling, 'Why didn't you tell me this before?' What he did say was, 'Did Penny go to bed, Granny?'

She shook her head, then pointed to a door leading out of the kitchen, which was where Daisy slept, and she said, 'They're both in there, she wouldn't go upstairs alone.'

He nodded at her; then lay down.

'Wake up, Eddie.'

Eddie! Eddie! Eddie! Eddie! Eddie! The sea was roaring through his head; he was drowning; he was struggling with someone; he was going to die, like his grandfather had died; and there was that fellow in the peaked cap again, dancing round him.

'Wake up, Eddie!'

When he sat bolt upright on the settle his grandmother stepped quickly back, exclaiming, 'That's it! scald me now.'

'Oh! Oh, Gran!' He was gasping as if he were still in the water. He must have been dreaming; but what a dream! He'd dreamt he was drowning, like his grandfather had drowned. Why . . . why should he dream that? . . . And that fellow again.

'Here, drink this, it's daylight.' As he took the mug of tea from his grandmother's hands, she said, 'What is it, what's the matter? You're shivering. Are you cold?'

He shook his head. He couldn't be bothered to reach for the trumpet and say he'd had another sort of nightmare. He took two or three gulps at the hot tea, then swung his feet down to the floor and his head drooped on to his chest for a moment. Oh Lord, but he felt tired. He couldn't remember ever feeling so tired.

'What?' He looked up at his grandmother.

'Will you go out and look again? If there's no sign of him I'm going into the town.'

'Yes, Grandma.' He rose to his feet.

'It's a rough morning; it's raining and the wind's blowing. The weather's coming in with the tide. There's an oilskin in the cupboard in the hall, put it on.'

He turned from her and went out of the kitchen and into the hall, and as he got into the stiff oilskins he thought, Where do I start? Where do I look? It would be much better if she went straight to the police station now.

As he entered the kitchen again, Daisy was coming out of her room; she was yawning widely and her eyes were full of sleep, but on the sight of him, she said, 'You didn't find him then?' And when he shook his head, she said, 'It's as the missis says, there's something fishy afoot and I'd like to bet me bottom dollar Mr Hal's in it.'

The mention of Hal Kemp's name made Eddie pause as he was going out of the back door. Should he tell his grandmother where his granda had gone yesterday afternoon and put up with her reactions? It was a strain to talk to her about anything and at the moment he certainly didn't feel up to it, he was so blooming tired. He would tell her when he came back. By then the wind would likely have blown the cobwebs out of his mind, but at the moment he didn't seem able to think clearly.

The rain wasn't heavy but the wind was high and blowing in from the sea and it carried the mournful sound of a ship's horn to him. He stood peering over the wet grass and down the slope towards the edge of the cliff. His grandfather couldn't have fallen over. No, of course not. He tossed his head at the mere idea. What would make his grandfather walk along that slope when he was always warning him and Penny to be careful of it? But further along the cliff top where the road almost touched the edge. What about there?

He turned his steps in the direction by which he had come home a few hours earlier, and now he walked as near the edge of the cliff as he considered safe. Every now and again he stopped and looked over, but there was no sign of a huddled form lying on the sands, or among the rocks, but from this point his view of the coastline, to the far left of him, was interrupted by the cliff jutting out towards the sea.

It was when he was about to turn towards home again that his attention was caught by a boat lying some way offshore. It wasn't the fact of the boat alone that made him continue to stare at it, because it was no unusual sight to see boats dotted here and there far out on the waters doing a bit of inshore fishing, but there was a sculler bobbing up and down near this boat and there were men seemingly busy on the deck of the boat and in the sculler too.

He rubbed the rain from his eyes, narrowed them and strained his gaze forward. They were dropping a big package into the sculler. Almost immediately the sculler was being rowed away from the boat, and towards ... where? From where he was standing he judged that the sculler was making for the cove below the house, the cove that seemed to belong to the house; it was the only sheltered cove on this stretch. He had only once been round there and he didn't like it; he'd had to drop down over the groyne that Daisy had told him about and he had thought the place had an awesome feeling.

Half-way down the cliffs the rocks jutted well out from the rest of the coastline. Yet the beach itself was narrow.

The foot of the rocks had been scalloped here and there into small caves, all shallow with the exception of one. This one he had stood inside and looked upwards to where a cleft had split the rock, probably half-way up the cliff face, for it showed a thread of daylight. A water mark running round the inside of the cave indicated that the tide reached almost up to his own head and he judged that it was from here the sound of the sea carried into the house because it must be almost in a straight line with it.

Had his grandfather been fishing all night after all and was coming home the shortest way? Eeh! He wouldn't like to be him when he entered the house, his granny would eat him alive.

He was now running back along the cliffpath, but when it veered away from the edge and dropped into the little valley he left and continued along the cliff where the land was still flat. That was until he saw the sculler being beached.

Coming to an abrupt stop, he wiped the rain from his face and stood peering down towards the beach. Ahead of him was a windswept stunted bush; it was situated about a hundred yards from where the cliff top began to slope steeply away. When he reached the bush he knelt down on to the sodden grass and, keeping his head low and close to the twisted branches, he peered forward. As he did so his breath caught in his throat and he seemed to hold it there as he watched two men lifting the package from the sculler. For what he had imagined to be a package was a man, a man all limp and dangling.

He couldn't make out, from this distance, and because of the rain, if the man had white hair and a beard, but whom he did make out and recognize was one of the men.

They had beached the sculler well up the little cove because the tide was running in swiftly, and within seconds of lifting the burden from it they disappeared from his view. But they seemed no sooner gone than they were back, and it was something about the way the second man pushed the boat off and jumped in that confirmed Eddie's belief that this man was Hal Kemp.

What must he do?

Go back to the house and tell his granny? But they couldn't get into the cove from the beach . . . and he couldn't swim round that groyne, he could hardly swim at all. Half a dozen breast strokes and he was finished. All that water in the river and he had never learnt to swim properly. He shook his head at himself.

Should he dash back into the town?

No, it was too far, for by the time he got there and they got a boat out the cave would be full.

He stayed no longer to think, but found himself racing inland towards the house.

When he reached the yard he skidded on the stones and nearly fell on to his face, and then thrusting open the top half of the kitchen door he grappled with the latch on the lower half, then tumbled into the kitchen.

For a moment he stood gasping and unable to speak as he looked from his granny to the man standing near the table. He looked at him as if he were an apparition, a good apparition, for it was Mr Reade.

'What is it, boy? What is it?' His grandmother had him by the shoulders, and he gulped in his throat and, thrusting his arm back to the kitchen door, he stabbed his finger towards it before he managed to bring out, 'A man! They've dumped a man in the cove just below. They ... they brought him in a sculler ... two men ... from a bigger boat ...'

'Get your breath, lad. Take it easy.' It was Mr Reade who now had hold of his shoulder. 'You say they've dumped somebody in the cove? Did you see who it was?'

'Aye. Well, I'm not sure. I don't know who the man was that they dumped. It might be –' He glanced at his grandmother, then turned his face to the side as he added, 'Me granda, but I think I recognized one of the men in the sculler. It was

Hal Kemp. You know, who lives here. And I know me granda went looking for him yesterday because of something I told him about Hal Kemp. I found out he was up to something with the Belgian man.'

When his granny pulled him round to face her and said, 'You think it's your granda down there, and Hal Kemp dumped him?' he didn't at first question why she should have apparently heard him.

'Yes, Grandma.'

'My God! But why? Why? . . . The tide . . . the tide's in.'

He watched her as she pressed her fingers tightly over her mouth then cupped her face with her two hands. When she looked towards Ted Reade he shook his head and said, 'I couldn't get a boat round there in time, Maggie; if he's out helpless he could be drowned. The only way is down the cliff. Have you any rope, long rope, strong?'

He was looking at Eddie now, but before Eddie could answer his granny said, 'There's no rope long enough and there's no stay on that slope to hold a rope.' She now closed her eyes tightly for a moment as she gripped her brow with one hand. Then she looked from one to the other and said, 'What must be, must be. Come this way, both of you.'

She was running now, up the kitchen and across the hall, but as she went to mount the stairs she turned her head to where Daisy was coming out of the dining room and she cried at her, 'If . . . if anybody comes, Hal Kemp or anybody, say I'm in me bed, bad.'

'In your bed bad, missis?'

'Yes, girl, just that, in me bed bad. Don't forget,

I'm in me bed bad and I can't see anybody.' And on this she ran up the stairs as if the years had fallen from her and she was a young woman once more.

By the time he entered his granny's bedroom, closely followed by Mr Reade, it seemed to Eddie that his mind had ceased to function, except that it told him that perhaps he was still in the nightmare, because if he wasn't mistaken his granny had certainly heard what he had said when he had his face turned from her; and she had also heard Daisy right across the hall. But now she was turning towards Mr Reade and, her words tumbling over each other, she said, 'Ted, swear to me here and now on this.' Reaching out she grabbed a Bible from the bedside table and thrust it into his hand. 'Swear to me, what you're going to see will be kept to yourself. No matter what happens it will be kept to yourself.'

'Well, if you want it that way, Maggie, I'll swear, but you needn't bid me swear on the Bible. I've trusted you afore this so I think you can trust me now.'

As she nodded at him she answered, 'Aye, you're right, Ted. You're right.'

She can hear. She can hear as well as me. Eeh! the old faggot. But why? why had she pretended to be deaf?

Eddie had no time to give any kind of answer to his own question for now all other thoughts were wiped away from his mind as he watched what his granny was doing; and as his eyes became round with amazement he was sure now that he was dreaming and it was all part of that nightmare, because his grandmother had gone into the cupboard that ran along the side of the room, and right opposite to him to the side of the bed the wall was moving, it was swivelling round . . .

Eeh! my!

'Go in, both of you, but stay still near the wall.'

Mr Reade's eyes were as wide as Eddie's as they stood side by side against a wall. They couldn't have hoped to have stood abreast because the place in which they were standing wasn't any more than two feet wide.

Eddie now watched his grandmother, who was holding a lamp in one hand, move a lever that was head high and as she pulled it downwards the door slid back into place.

Mr Reade now followed his granny and he followed Mr Reade, and, his mouth open and his eyebrows stretching to meet his hairline, he gazed about him. They had taken no more than three steps along the narrow passage and now they were in a long, narrow room, a doorless room, but one which was furnished. At the very far end he made out the shape of a bed, and nearer the middle was a table and two chairs, and against a wall was a book rack that held a number of books; next to it, a small writing desk. But at his feet, and his eyes became riveted on them, a number of steps dropped into deep blackness.

'Here!' His granny was holding out a candle to him and one to Mr Reade. 'It's too dangerous to take the lamp, and if one of us drops a candle, well, we can always get a light from the others. Now do what I tell you, because . . . well, there's places that if you put a foot wrong it could be your last. An' I mean that, Ted.'

'Aye, Maggie, just as you say.'

'Well, come on.' Carefully now, she eased herself through the hole in the floor and onto the steps below, and then, when her head was just visible above the floor she continued, 'Hold tight to the rope banister, the steps are slippery.'

And they *were* slippery. More than once Eddie felt his feet almost give way under him. The stairway was no wider than the passage that led from the bedroom and was so steep it seemed almost vertical.

He breathed a sigh of relief when he reached the bottom and into what looked like a room similar to the one above. But his relief was short lived, for his granny was pointing down to another hole and saying, 'The steps on this part are few and far between, it's mostly slope, and at one point where it narrows you'll have to walk sideways. But I'll tell you when we come to it.' And without further words she went forward and down.

And down. And down. And down.

Eddie knew that they must be somewhere inside the actual cliff, yet he had the weird feeling that they were descending into the bowels of the earth.

'Now.'

Obeying his granny's order, he turned sideways and although he himself passed easily through the aperture he saw that Mr Reade had had to pull his stomach in.

His granny was standing still now, the candle

held high, and, pointing ahead, she said, 'The passage widens further along but stick close to this side of the wall, especially at the widest part where the loop is. Anyway, just follow me closely.' And on this she went ahead again.

Eddie hadn't to be told to stick close to the wall; the place was giving him the creeps, and he grabbed at it as he went along and his bewildered mind was noting two things; it wasn't slimy as he would have expected it to be, and the air down here wasn't foisty. It was neither hot nor cold, but there was a constant roar of noise and it was getting louder every minute.

Ooh!

The passage had suddenly widened out and he was following Mr Reade around the loop – and it was a loop, like three parts of a circle – and there just at the place where they would have stepped had they walked straight on was a hole, and partly covering it were two planks of wood. But up from its depths was coming a concerted roar as if it were a pit full of wild animals.

His stomach gave a heave as he came to the end of the loop for now his feet were within a foot of the edge of the hole. He had never felt fear like this before. He had the desire to cry out aloud, like a frightened bairn would, or pray. He did neither, for his granny was yelling, 'Watch your feet! It's a slope. Hang on to the rope!'

He hung on to the rope, clutching at it as if his life depended on it as his feet almost gave way beneath him. Then of a sudden his fear left him for it was swamped by fresh amazement. He was in a cave, a big cave, and it was full of candles;

they were strewn all over the floor, bursting out of boxes, thousands upon thousands of candles. They were treading on them.

His gaze was brought to his granny now where she was lifting a rope ladder from a hook in the rock wall. Handing it to Ted Reade, she said, 'Do you think it will hold, it's many years since it was used?'

Eddie watched Mr Reade tugging and pulling at the black tarred rope; then he nodded and said, 'Except for the ends it's still good.'

Now both he and Eddie watched her go to the wall of the rock from where protruded a lever similar to the one that closed the stone wall up above. But as her hand gripped it she turned and looked over her shoulder at Ted Reade and, her breath coming in gasps, she said, 'You'd better help me, it'll take some opening. It's like the ladder, it's many a year since it's been used.'

'Which way does it turn?'

'You push it up, then around, a full half-moon.'

He was a strong man was Ted Reade, but when he went to push the lever he couldn't budge it.

'Oh my God!' The agonized words brought Eddie's eyes to his granny again and as he went quickly forward to add his strength to that of Mr Reade he almost slipped on the candle-strewn floor; instinctively he stooped down, and picking up a handful of squashed tallow and cords, he turned to his granny and said, 'Perhaps it wants a grease?'

'Aye, yes.' She nodded quickly, and Ted Reade grabbed the tangled mass from Eddie's hand and rammed it round the joint of the lever. Then applying all his strength to it, he pushed once more. There was a small grinding movement and the iron handle slowly inched forward, then stopped. Again Ted rubbed in more grease and again he pushed the lever, this time with Eddie's fist next to his. And now, creaking and groaning, the lever moved its required half circle, and as it did so there was a grinding and screeching as if stones were being crushed in a mill as a narrow slab of rock slowly edged inwards, leaving an aperture about four feet high and two feet wide; and on its opening the thunder of the sea as it roared into the cave enveloped them.

Eddie was straining to see over his grandmother's shoulder where she knelt on the floor looking downwards into the cave, when her cry, which was higher than the wind, startled him: '*Davy! Davy!* He's there! He's there!'

As she knelt back Ted looked over her head and down into the cave and what he said was, 'Aye, my God! he's there all right.'

'Get by a minute.' His granny was screaming now, and they jumped aside and stood and watched as she took the two hooks that were attached to the rope ladder and clipped them into staples one on each side of the aperture; then throwing the ladder out into the cave, she shouted, 'You'll both have to go down. If you can lift him up I'll get him in.'

Eddie had no time to register further amazement for now, following Ted, he found himself climbing from the aperture, which was flush with the cave wall, down the inside of the cave.

He shuddered as the cold water flooded his

boots but his own discomfort was soon lost in the emotion he felt as he looked down on his grandfather, his white hair red with blood, his beard matted, his face grey. He looked lifeless.

As Ted put his arms under the old man's shoulder and hoisted him upwards he yelled, 'I don't see how we're going to lift him up there. We want a sling, a rope or something.' He yelled now above the sound of the wind and lashing water.

'Have you a rope, Maggie? We want a rope!'

His grandmother's face disappeared for a moment; then she was looking down at them again and yelling, 'There's none here. But wait, wait, there's one at the loop.'

'Laddie' – Ted was shouting again – 'help to hold him upright out of the water till I feel if he's breathin'.'

Using all his strength now to support the drooping figure of his grandfather, Eddie watched Mr Reade pulling open his grandfather's jacket and waistcoat and thrusting his hand inside them. And when he nodded deeply at him, then yelled, 'He's a tough 'un, he'll take some killin', but somebody's done his damnest to bring it off,' Eddie drew in a sharp relieving breath.

When the coil of rope fell, it hit Eddie on the head, but he made no protest; he just held on to his grandfather as Ted looped the rope under his arms.

'I'll go up first,' Ted yelled now. 'And pray to God this ladder'll hold. You push on his feet from the bottom, lad; that'll take some of the weight. All right?'

'All right.'

Eddie, pushing with one hand on the soles of his grandfather's boots, while clinging desperately to the swaying rope ladder with the other, unconsciously paid tribute to his training in the shipyard where climbing almost vertical ladders was part of his daily work. But in this present case the pace was so slow he imagined they were climbing the complete cliff face. Then when he thought his arms would break, of a sudden the pressure was gone, and he heaved a sigh of relief as he saw his grandfather's legs disappearing into the aperture. The next minute he was at the top of the ladder and into the cave himself, there to hear his grandmother crying, 'Oh Davy! Davy! Oh my God! Who's done this to you?'

She was kneeling by the side of his grandfather now and she turned and looked up at Ted, saying, 'He was the kindest man on earth, who would do this to him? Surely not Hal? He's been so good to Hal; he didn't like him but he's been good to him.'

'Get up, Maggie.' Ted raised Mrs Flannagan to her feet, saying as he did so, 'Somebody wanted him out of the way, that's sure. But why? That's the question. There wasn't a better man livin' than him. But now we've got to get him to bed, Maggie, and as quick as possible. An' that's gona be easier said than done, for we're gona have our work cut out to get him back up that treacherous passage ... Whoever cut that out wasn't thinkin' of comfort. And there's that door.' He pointed towards the gap in the rock. 'I'd better close it.'

A few minutes later he was standing by Mrs Flannagan again and she was looking up at him, saying, 'You'll go easy with him, Ted?'

'We'll go easy with him, Maggie. You go on ahead an' give us light.'

'Can you manage his legs, lad?'

'Yes, I'll manage his legs.'

Eddie waited a moment as Ted heaved the limp body upwards with the back towards him, then with his arms under the old man's oxters and around his chest, he said, 'Right?' and Eddie answered, 'Right,' before taking in a deep breath, and stooping, gripped each of his grandfather's legs in the crook of his arms. And so the perilous journey began.

Ted had of necessity to walk backwards and trust in Mrs Flannagan's hand on his shoulder to guide his steps.

They rested three times before they reached the loop, stopping immediately they came upon the awe inspiring hole, and again when they were past it.

The journey seemed to be never ending and became almost impossible when they had to press and pull his grandfather through the narrowest part of the passage, but his fear, Eddie realized, had left him once they had passed the roaring hole.

However, both he and Ted were nearing the end of their strength when they reached the lower room and the foot of the steps, and as they rested for a moment Mrs Flannagan, her voice holding a pleading note, said, 'One last effort, Ted.'

It seemed unfair to Eddie in this moment that

his granny hadn't yet recognized his part in the effort. But what did it matter? That would be the day when he got a word of appreciation from his granny. The main thing now was to get his granda up this last flight of steps.

When he heard his granny say, 'Lay him on there, Ted,' as she pointed towards the bed in the far corner of the cave room, he showed no surprise, for his main concern now was to lay his part of the burden down before his arms snapped.

'On there, Maggie?' Ted's words came out between gasps.

'Aye, for the present.'

When they had laid Mr Flannagan on what, on closer inspection, Eddie saw to be a very narrow single bed, more like a couch, he stood panting and rubbing at his arms while he watched his grandmother examine the wound on his grandfather's head, then open his coat and lay her ear to his chest. And with fresh amazement he again thought, Eeh! she can hear as well as me, the old twister. But why the trumpet?

His mind hadn't time to give himself any answer to the question before his granny said, 'The cuts are not deep, and his heart's going strong, thank God ... Would you get his coat and trousers off for me? I'll be back in a minute.' And with this she hurried down the room and from their view. But she was back again within a few minutes, her arms laden with bedding and night clothes.

'He'll likely get his death in here, won't he, Maggie?'

Mrs Flannagan shook her head at Ted as, with

her own hands, she stripped off the wet vest and pants from her husband's body; then both Eddie and Ted went to her aid when she attempted to dress him in the thick flannel night-shirt. This done, she indicated that he should be rolled on to his side so that she could put blankets underneath him. And not until he was wrapped warmly in the bedding did she straighten her back and say, 'The temperature never varies in here, it's neither hot nor cold, and there's no damp. No one has ever got rheumatism through laying on that bed.

'Now –' She patted her cheek twice with her hand before going towards a tall-backed chair and dropping onto it. Looking from one to the other, she said, 'I've been thinking. On the journey back I've been thinking a lot, Ted. To my mind whoever did this to him had a purpose. As I see it they wanted him to be found down there in the cave; his body having been dashed against the rocks in the confined space would account for the blood on him and the crack on his head.' . . .

She paused and Ted said, 'I'm not followin' you, Maggie. Why should they want him to be found down there?'

'Because if they had dumped him in the river, it's ten to one he would have come back with the tide after three days and it could have looked like foul play and the polis could have worked back to those he was seen with last. But on the other hand, being found on his own property, so to speak, they could put it down to him falling asleep down there – he walked the beach a lot, you know that, Ted – or that he was waiting for a

boat coming in, a certain type of boat' – she
nodded her head at him – 'and he was cut off by
the tide. Or they would just say he was drunk; it
was well known he liked his drop. So from what
the lad here saw down on the beach' – she indicated Eddie with a motion of her hand – 'my
smooth-tongued nephew is in this up to the neck.
As I see it, when they send somebody to stroll
along the beach and come up on him accidentally' – she put out her hand and touched the
bed – 'and they don't find any body they'll think
he did go out with the tide. So Ted, I mean to bide
my time and see what transpires, and give them
enough rope to hang themselves. By then, please
God, I'll know what all this is about, for when he
comes round he'll put some light on the matter.
But in the meantime he'll have to have a doctor.
Would you go and ask Doctor Collington to pay
me a visit, Ted? Tell him I'm very much under the
weather.'

'You mean old Collington? But he's been
retired these eight years or more, Maggie.'

'Retired or not, he'll come, Ted. Just say to
him, "Maggie Flannagan needs you," and he'll be
here as quick as his trap will bring him.'

Ted kept his clear blue eyes on her for a
moment before nodding and saying, 'Just as you
say, Maggie, just as you say. I'll be away then.'

'Thanks, Ted. And I've no need to ask you not
to forget your oath?'

Ted's countenance was stiff as he replied,
'Now, Maggie, I think you should know me better
than that.'

'Aye, Ted; I'm sorry.'

As Mrs Flannagan rose, saying, 'I'll see you through,' Eddie cleared his throat before blurting out, 'I think there's something more you should know, Gran, an' you an' all, Mr Reade.'

They both turned now and stared at him, and he swallowed again before he said, 'Well, it's like this . . .' And he went back to the happening on Wednesday evening and the conversation with his grandfather yesterday dinner-time.

'Why didn't you tell me this last night?' His grandmother's voice was recognizable by its old tone.

'Well, you were so troubled, so worried, and at the same time I didn't think for one minute that Hal Kemp would be bad enough to do anything to me granda.'

'That fellow, Mr Van, as you call him' – Ted was nodding now – 'gentleman like. Aye. Aye, when you come to think of it it's makin' sense, fittin' in. I saw him one day last week comin' off Abel Denkin's boat. Now what would a gentleman like him be doing with the like of Abel Denkin 'cos, you know, Maggie' – he was now nodding at her – 'there's runnin' and runnin'. A drop that warms you on a winter's night is one thing, but there are other things not so pleasant. An' I've been hearin' rumours of late.' He now nodded towards the bed and said, 'You're right, Maggie; there's something fishy about all this, and the Captain must have cottoned on to it. Anyway, trust me; I'll keep both me eyes and ears open.'

'Thanks, Ted.' The worried lines on her face softened as she ended now, 'You're like the answer to a prayer. I don't know where we would have turned the night if it hadn't been for you because me and the lad here' – she inclined her head towards Eddie – 'we would never have got him up out of that cove on our own.'

'No, that's right, Maggie. But when we're dishin' out thanks' – his face broadened into a smile now – 'we would never have known he was in the cove, would we, if it hadn't been for the lad there. Now, would we?'

'No, no; you're right there.'

Eddie blinked as his grandmother turned her face fully towards him. But she didn't say, 'Thank you, lad,' what she said was, 'Go down to the kitchen and tell Daisy to fill the four stone bottles, and you bring an oven shelf up, that's if' – she paused and her voice became bitter – 'the prodigal son hasn't returned. Well, if he's there just give Daisy the message. Tell her I'm cold; and forget about the oven shelf and keep him talking, even fighting. And that shouldn't be difficult for you, should it?'

Even when her lips twisted into a wry smile he thought, Eeh! she's still the same, trumpet or no trumpet.

Mrs Flannagan now rose from the chair and followed them both through the aperture into the bedroom and as she went towards the bedroom door to let them out, she paused; then taking hold of Eddie's arm, she quickly drew him back towards the head of the bed, saying, 'I'll keep that closed,' and thumbed towards the aperture in the rock wall. Pointing to a square of stone above the bedhead, which looked no different from the others except that it was so placed that the end of it was in line with the end of the bed rail, she added, 'Knock on that. It's a single slab, I'll hear you ... Yes' – she nodded briskly at him now – 'I know what you're thinking, but keep it to yourself for the present. And I repeat, I'll *hear* you. Go on now.' She almost pushed him from her.

He felt his indignation rising. It seemed unfair the way she treated him. After all he had gone through during the last few hours, she still acted towards him as if he were a bairn, and an unruly one at that ...

Hal Kemp wasn't in the kitchen. It was three o'clock that afternoon before he came into the house, by which time many things had happened. An old man carrying a black hard case bag had gone through his grandmother's bedroom and into that strange, weird place and hadn't blinked an eyelid. He had examined his grandfather and pronounced that he had concussion. He had stitched the wound in his head, then had drunk half a tumbler of brandy that his granny offered him. And all the while he had called his granny, Maggie, and she had called him, Stephen. It was as if they had known each other intimately all their lives. On leaving, he had said the first thing he would do when he got back to town would be to inform the police of the captain's disappearance; and he added, 'I'll be back in the morning, Maggie.'

... And Daisy. Daisy's questioning had caused him more bother than the policeman's. What was

103

going on up there? The mistress was in her nightie and in bed all right but where were the four water bottles, the bed was as flat as a pancake? And why had they all previously been so long in the bedroom, and the bedroom door locked? Wouldn't he tell her what was going on? She had appealed to him; he could trust her.

Looking back now he remembered his surprise at his reaction when she had said he could trust her: he had put his hand on her shoulder and, leaning towards her, had said quietly, 'I know I can, Daisy; and if it only lay with me I would tell you everything. But you'll likely know soon enough, so will you trust me and ask no more questions and do just what I tell you?'

Another time he would have expected her answer to be explosive, but she had further surprised him by saying softly, 'All right, Eddie; only . . . only look after yourself 'cos I'm sort of frightened inside. I don't know why, but I'm just frightened inside.'

As he gazed down into her face a strangely protective feeling towards her had come over him. Then straightening his shoulders, he had said, 'There's nothing for you to be afraid of.' And almost without pausing he had asked, 'Where's Penny?'

Her reply, 'Out in the stable. She found a seagull on the cliff top with its wing broken,' had caused him to dash out of the house and rush to the stable.

There, he had caught hold of Penny and, to her amazement and indignation, almost dragged her into the kitchen and shouted at her, 'Now you stay along of Daisy! Don't go wandering on those cliff tops. Do you hear me?'

She had burst out crying, exclaiming as she did so, 'What's got into you, our Eddie? Oh, I wish me ma was back. Oh! I do. I do.' And he had endorsed this loudly, crying, 'And so do I! It's one body's work lookin' after you.'

At this both girls gaped at him, and he had turned from their stares and marched out of the room, saying to no one in particular, 'Oh yes, I wish me ma was back. There's nobody wishes that more than me.'

6

The wind was high again and likely this was why neither Eddie, nor Daisy, nor Penny heard Hal Kemp's footsteps in the yard. It wasn't until he snapped up the latch of the lower part of the door that they were aware of him.

Eddie was at the fire about to lift the big black kettle off the hob in order to refill the hot water bottles, and he didn't turn round but his hand remained still on the handle of the kettle, until the fierce heat of the fire made him jerk it from the hob and on to the fender.

His granny had told him to act natural. Well, now was the time to start; but for the life of him he couldn't turn round and face that man at the moment without his feelings giving him away, and so he was grateful when he heard Penny say, 'Oh, hello, Uncle Hal. We were wondering where you had got to.'

When Hal Kemp's answer came it sounded quiet, very unlike his usual boisterous tone. 'Been fishin' . . . There!'

There was a soft thud on the table which proclaimed to Eddie that Hal Kemp had brought evidence of his fishing trip.

'Where's Auntie?'

It was Daisy who answered now, saying, 'She's bad, in bed.'

'Bad, in bed?'

'Aye, that's what I said. She had to have the doctor this mornin' ... It's worry over the master.'

There was a pause before Hal Kemp asked, 'What do you mean, worry over the master?'

It took all Eddie's self-control to go on filling the water bottles, for he had the greatest urge to turn round and spring at the man and beat him to the ground. He could see himself jumping on him and punching him until he was in the same state as he had left an old man this morning.

'The captain's lost.'

Again there was a pause before Hal Kemp said, 'What you talking about, girl?'

'Just what I said, the captain's lost. He went out yesterday and hasn't come back. The polis has been.'

'The polis, here?' There had been no pause before this question.

'Aye, not one, but two. And the coastguard an' all.'

There was silence in the kitchen for a moment, broken only by the sound of Eddie screwing the stone stoppers into the water bottles; and not until he had tested them, to see that they weren't running out, by turning each bottle on to its end did he turn about and look at the man standing now at the far side of the kitchen table.

As Hal Kemp returned Eddie's look he seemed to regain a little of his own sarcastic

107

boisterousness for now he exclaimed, 'Changin'
your trade, lad, playin' nursemaid? You'd better
look out, Daisy' – he nodded towards Daisy who
was staring at him, her face straight – 'else you'll
be losing your job.'

What Eddie's response to this would have been
he didn't know. Yet of one thing he was certain, it
wouldn't have been in accordance with his
granny's orders. But his impulse was checked by
a violent dig in the back and Daisy yelling at him,
'If you don't take those bottles upstairs they'll be
as cold as dish water. Go on, don't stand there
like a stook.'

Daisy's pushing had caused him to take a few
steps past the table and when he swung round
she was close behind him with her back to Hal
Kemp, and it was the look on her face, the warning in her eyes, that checked his outburst; and so,
almost flinging himself round again, he went
from the room, across the hall, took the stairs two
at a time, crossed the landing at a run, only on
reaching his grandmother's door to tap gently on
it twice.

Almost immediately, it was opened and his
granny, dressed in a long white nightdress that
was buttoned under her chin and which fell to the
floor and covered her slippers, pulled him into the
room, saying, 'I know, I know. I saw him coming,
from the window. Bring them in quick!' She went
ahead of him through the aperture in the wall,
along the narrow passage, and into the wall room,
saying as she went, 'He's awake, he's spoken. Put
that one at his feet.' She now grabbed the other
water bottle from Eddie and, lifting the blankets,

put it gently against her husband's side, murmuring as she did so, 'There you are, Davy. There you are, man. Keep warm, sweat it out. I'll be back in a minute. Lie quiet now.'

With that, she patted her husband's cheek that was no longer pale but flushed and a deep red. Then taking Eddie by the arm, she turned him about and drew him back into the bedroom. She then went into the cupboard, and Eddie stood and watched the wall move into place, and he marvelled that once it was settled it looked as if it had never been moved.

Sitting on the side of the bed, his granny now threw off her slippers, revealing her stockinged feet and the fact that she was fully dressed underneath, and, getting into bed, she drew Eddie to her with a motion of her hand. And now she whispered to him, 'If I know anything he'll be up here in a minute, so stay by me because, like you, I'm not very good at acting, and also playing the hypocrite; and what's more I don't want to be left alone with him because God knows what I might be tempted to do.'

Eddie nodded at her. He could understand her feelings and strangely at this moment he felt very close to her. She was no longer the old vixen with the ear trumpet, and she had asked him to stand by her. He leaned towards her now, saying with a mischievous glint in his eye, 'You'd better remember you're still deaf.'

She now pressed her lips tightly together and slanted her eyes at him, but she said nothing, only reached out and, picking up the ear trumpet from the side table, she laid it on the counterpane.

But when he said, 'I'd better unbolt the door,' she nodded to him.

He had hardly withdrawn the bolt when he heard the heavy footsteps on the oak stairs. He turned and signalled to his grandmother, and she in turn signalled back to him to take the seat by the side of the bed.

When the voice came from beyond the door calling loudly, 'All right to come in, Auntie?' they exchanged glances, and Eddie saw it was with a great effort that his grandmother forced herself not to reply, but nodded furiously at him. And so it was he who called out, 'Aye; it's all right.'

The door opened and Hal Kemp entered the room. After closing the door behind him, he paused a moment and shook his head as he looked towards the bed. Then moving slowly forward, he said, 'Oh, Aunt Maggie, what's happened to you?'

'What?' She had her trumpet to her ear.

'What's happened to you?'

'A cold.' The suppressed emotion in her voice even caused her to croak.

'Oh, I'm sorry. And' – again he was shouting into the trumpet – 'what's this I hear about Uncle not comin' home yet? Has he gone out with some of his cronies on a fishing trip, do you think?'

His granny was so long in answering that Eddie, feeling she was about to let loose her pent up feelings on her nephew, moved his legs and accidentally on purpose brought his knee in sharp contact with the mattress.

'I shouldn't think so, not from what the constable said.'

'Well, I shouldn't worry; he's likely sleeping it

off somewhere. It won't be the first time that he's stayed out all night.'

'What do you mean?'

'Well, if he's had a load on he might have woken up with a head and wanted to get over it afore he faced you. Perhaps he's havin' a hair of the dog that bit him to bolster up his courage.'

He'd hardly finished the last word before the trumpet was grabbed from his hand.

'Get out and leave me alone!'

'Aw well, if you're feelin' like that I'll go.' But before turning from the bed he leaned towards her and mouthed, 'I'll have a walk along the coastline. Who knows but he may have hurt himself or something.'

'What do you say?' He turned a steely gaze on Eddie who, looking back at him, muttered, 'Nowt.'

'Well, it better be nowt, laddie. And what are you sittin' up here for anyway?' He had turned from the bed now but continued to talk as he walked towards the door. 'Gettin' on the right side of the old girl, are you? Hoping for rewards for being a good boy?'

The door knob in his hand, he turned and looked towards the bed, and what he saw brought his mouth slightly open and his eyes narrowing because Mrs Flannagan's arm was stretched across the coverlet and her hand was gripping Eddie's wrist, the sleeve of her nightdress had fallen back and the cuff and part of the sleeve of her grey housedress was showing. He continued to stare at them both for some few seconds before turning swiftly and going out. And they heard

111

his footsteps crossing the landing and the opening and shutting of his bedroom door.

Mrs Flannagan's hand was still holding Eddie's wrist and they both looked down at it, and, pointing to the cuff of her dress, she whispered, 'Do you think he noticed that?'

'Aye, I think so,' he whispered back.

'It's just as well then.' She nodded at him. 'We'll see what happens next. If he thinks we're on to him it won't be long before he shows his hand in some way. Bolt the door again. Do it quietly.'

Within a matter of seconds she was out of the bed, in and out of the oak cupboard, and was passing through the opening into the wall room. Eddie followed as quickly and saw her smile as she approached the bed, for Mr Flannagan's eyes were wide open; and when she caught hold of his hand he said, 'Maggie! Maggie!'

'Yes, Davy, what is it? How you feeling?'

'Maggie.'

'Yes, dear.'

'How . . . how did I get . . . here?'

'It's a long story. We'll tell you all about it later. Here, drink this.' She held a cup to his lips.

After he had sipped at it his head drooped back on the pillow and he closed his eyes, saying, 'It's painful, Maggie. It's painful.'

'Yes, dear, but it's all right. Stephen's been. He stitched you up; you're going to be all right.'

'Stephen?'

'Aye.'

'Why . . . why am I not in my own bed, Maggie?'

'A number of reasons, Davy. But you'll be there soon. Can ... can you tell us what happened?'

'What?' He screwed up his eyes against the pain in his head, then said, 'I ... I can't think; this flaming pain.'

'All right, don't worry, just lie quiet. Go to sleep.' She gently stroked his brow.

They sat one on each side of him until he had fallen asleep again, then she motioned to Eddie and they moved from the room and back into the bedroom, and there, flopping down on to the side of the bed, she said, 'I'm very tired, boy, and you must be the same. Once he gets out of the house' – she pointed a weary hand towards the bedroom door – 'we must have a rest, if it's only for an hour or so, because I've got a feeling that this business is just at the beginning.'

'Gran.'

'Yes, boy?'

'How will you go about telling them that you've had granda here all the time?'

She nodded her head slowly; and then she answered, 'I've given that some thought meself, and I think the only thing I'll be able to say, and that only up till tomorrow, is that he fell into a ditch and banged his head on a rock and when he came to he stumbled home. But after tomorrow, well that wouldn't wash. I doubt if they'd believe it now. But give me time, I'll think of something. Only one thing is sure, they must never know about that' – she pointed to the open rock door – 'because if they ever found out there was such a place – not that they haven't had their

113

suspicions; oh aye – but if they ever got proof of it their memory would go back years, and from there they would pick up threads that would shatter a number of lives. So, boy, remember that you, too, are carrying a weight on your shoulders, the weight of a silent tongue. Even your mother who was brought up in this very house knows nothing about that place. List! ... There he goes.'

They both listened to the footsteps go across the landing and down the stairs; then his granny said, 'Stand by the side of the window and watch for him going.'

Eddie did as he was bid. But when five minutes had passed, then ten, he looked towards his granny and said, 'He must be having a meal. No!' – his head jerked quickly now – 'there he is. He's got a bundle with him.'

Almost as he finished speaking there was a knock on the door and Daisy's voice came to them, saying, 'Missis! Missis!'

All tiredness apparently gone from her, Mrs Flannagan seemed to spring to the cupboard and out again, and as she climbed into the bed the stone door fell into place. And now she nodded towards Eddie, and he, taking the signal, opened the door.

Daisy stood just within the room looking from one to the other. There was something going on and she wasn't part of it and her expression showed that she didn't like it.

Slowly she went to the foot of the bed and her hand moved round one of the knobs two or three times before she said, 'He's gone.'

'Gone? What do you mean, gone?'

'I mean Mr Hal's done a flit.'

'How do you make that out?'

'Well, he's broken the cash box in the desk in the sittin' room and taken the money out of it.'

'He's what!'

'What I said. I was in the hall when he came downstairs. He didn't see me but he went into the sittin' room and I heard him opening the desk. When he banged it closed I made for the kitchen, and when he came in he said, "I'm ... I'm off then, Daisy." '

She stopped here, and Mrs Flannagan said impatiently, 'Well, go on.'

'He asked me to go along with him.'

'He asked you to go ...!' Mrs Flannagan's mouth opened into a gape.

'Ah-ha.' She was nodding at her mistress now. 'He said what Mr Van had said, that he could get me a good place out in Belgium, Brussels.'

'Brussels?'

'Aye, missis, Brussels. It's an easy place to remember, like brussel sprouts.' She gave a little laugh; but then, her face becoming serious again, she went on, 'He offered me a whole half-sovereign. He said Mr Van had a nice house there and lovely children and I'd be set up for life, and ... and I'd be a fool if I didn't jump at it.'

Eddie looked from Daisy to his granny, who was sitting bolt upright in the bed now; and he couldn't understand the expression on his granny's face. She didn't look mad at Daisy, it was just as if what she had said had surprised her, shocked her like.

Daisy was gabbling now, 'I wouldn't have gone, missis, and I told him flat to his face. I told him that you had always been decent to me, sometimes as good as a mother, except when you had your tantrums like. Well, as I said to him when he told me to remember how you went at me, well, I said it was like water off a duck's back to me . . .'

'Daisy, come here.'

Daisy walked slowly to the bed now and her face showed surprise when her mistress caught hold of her hand and, shaking it up and down, said, 'You're a good lass, Daisy, you're a good lass, but listen to me, listen carefully. Now I know it's your time out the day but you said you'd stay in. By that you mean you're not going on the shore, or into the town, or along to Biddy's; but very often in the daytime you take a dander on the cliff top just to get a breath of fresh air. I know, I know, I'm not chastizing you.' She was nodding her head vigorously now. 'But what I want you to promise me is that you won't go beyond the yard until I tell you, you won't take a step further than that yard. Now promise me.'

'Aye, missis, aye, I'll promise you. Anyway, if I have a minute I prefer to put me feet up on the fender to warm me toes with the weather coming on as it is.'

'That's what to do, put your feet up on the fender and warm your toes.'

'Aye, missis, yes, I'll do that . . . Eeh! Eeh! missis, missis' – Daisy was now gulping in her throat and pointing to the side table on which lay the trumpet – 'you're hearin' me. Eeh!' She turned her bewildered gaze down on Eddie and repeated, 'She's hearin' me without it. It never struck me till now . . .'

Again her hand was caught and now slapped hard as her mistress in her old well-known raucous tone cried, 'Yes, I'm hearing you, Daisy Clinton, and I've been hearing you for the past six months, did you know it, ever since I came back from Newcastle. Now go on downstairs and think of all the things you said behind me back.'

Daisy walked backwards from the bed, then stopped and, her head wagging, she now said, 'Well, it won't affect me conscience none if I do, missis, 'cos I've never said anythin' behind your back that I haven't said to your face, I mean into your trumpet. Eeh! to think that all along you were only kiddin'.'

'There you're mistaken, girl, because all along I wasn't kidding. I've had partial hearing in this ear' – she pointed now to her left ear – 'for the past six months and it was because everybody said that it was useless going up there that I let them go on thinking it was useless. It served me purpose in many ways, and I found out who me friends were. Anyway, what was the good of shouting about it when they told me up there it may only be temporary and I could lose it at any time again. Anyway, go on now, get down those stairs. But remember what I told you, not to step further than the yard.'

'Aye, missis, aye.'

As Daisy went from the room she turned her head on her shoulder and looked back at Eddie, and the look was asking, What do you make of this?

When the door closed on her, Mrs Flannagan

beckoned to Eddie, saying, 'Come here, boy,' and when he stood by the side of the bed she said rapidly, 'Go down as quick as your legs will carry you and tell Ted Reade I want to see him. Tell him it's very important.'

'Aye, Gran; but . . . but what if he's gone out in his boat, will I get anybody else?'

'What do you say?' His granny now turned her head to the side and for the moment Eddie thought she was going to reach for the trumpet, but what she did was cup her ear with the palm of her hand and use it like a sucker. He was reminded of the one they had in the shipyard with which they cleared the pipes, and when of a sudden she said, 'Damn it!' he went hastily round the bed, and, picking up the trumpet from the table, he handed it to her, only to have it and his hand knocked roughly aside as she exclaimed, 'I don't want it. It'll come back, it's got to.' Her pumping became more vigorous now, and again she repeated, 'Damn it!' and added, 'Don't let them be right. Oh, anyway' – she pushed her hand out towards him – 'go on, get yourself away. And send Penny up here to me.'

She now swung her legs out of the bed and, her voice changing to an appeal, she said, 'Run, boy, run! because this is a serious business. That swine of a nephew of mine was right when he said he could be lynched for it.'

It was as if his granny's words had revived the feeling he'd had when just a short while ago he had rushed into the stable and dragged Penny into the kitchen, for now he ran from the room, down the stairs, through the hall and into the kitchen, and there, grabbing up his cap and coat, he shouted to Penny, who was sitting by the fire, 'Go on upstairs right away, Gran wants you. And you' – he stabbed his finger towards Daisy – 'do what she said, mind, don't move away from the yard. And don't even go there unless you have to.'

'What's it all about?'

'Never you mind, you'll know soon enough . . . at least I hope you won't.' And with this enigmatic reply, he ran from the kitchen, out of the yard, across the grass and on to the cliff path.

It was as he reached the path that he stopped and looked out to sea. There were a number of ships on the horizon and nearer to the shore a number of smaller craft, but they all seemed to be moving, with the exception of one. His eyes became riveted on this particular boat. Was it the same boat he had seen yesterday morning? A lot of fishing vessels and even bigger ones looked alike, but this particular one looked familiar and it was anchored.

Mr Reade . . . he must get Mr Reade, and it would soon be dark. Now, as if he had wings to his feet, he flew along the cliff path. This was the nearest way to the Lawe and the particular stretch of the waterfront beyond it.

His running was reduced to a trot by the time he reached the Lawe bank, and he took the last hundred yards at a walk before coming to Ted Reade's house.

After he had banged on the door twice it was opened, and an old woman faced him. 'Well!' she said; 'you seem in a hurry. What is it, lad?'

'Mr Reade.' He brought the name out on a gasp. 'Is . . . is he in?'

'No. No, lad. Well now' – she smiled broadly at him – ' 'tis Sunday afternoon and . . . and after a big dinner and a fill-up of beer afore that, he's usually upstairs at this time sleeping it off. But today he's taken a sculler across to North Shields, a bit of business he has to do there.' She nodded at him. 'Couldn't wait, he said, 'cos he's sailing out the night on the tide. Was it some fish you were wantin'?'

'No, no.' He shook his head. 'I'm . . . I'm Mrs Flannagan's grandson, and . . . and she wants him urgently.'

'Oh!' – the woman nodded at him now – 'Mrs Flannagan's grandson. Oh aye.' Again she nodded. 'Well now, he'll be sorry he's missed you 'cos he's fond of Maggie, he is that. But I tell you what.' She leant towards him. 'The minute he steps in the door I'll give him your message, an' if it's at all possible he'll be along those cliffs like a linty. Aye, like a linty.'

'Thanks.' He nodded and backed a couple of steps away from her, then added, 'You'll tell him it's very urgent, and . . . and me granny's very worried? She needs help.'

The woman's face was straight now and her voice had a sober tone as she said, 'I'll tell him your exact words, lad. I'll do more than that, I'll send somebody down to the quay so that when he comes in he doesn't linger, 'cos he's got to pass The Anchor an' who knows but he might drop in.'

'Ta. Thanks.'

'You're welcome, lad.'

He turned now and walked up the street.

What should he do? Go to the police? But the police were already looking for his granda, and if he told them what was in his mind with regard to the dreadful game he thought Hal Kemp and that Mr Van were up to they might just laugh at him and say he had been reading too many penny dreadfuls. But that's what he should do, he should go to the police.

Yet what proof had he? Only that the Belgian man had offered Daisy a job in his house. But there was proof enough that Hal Kemp and another had tried to murder his grandfather. If that came out though, it would put them all on their guard and they would scatter and likely carry on their terrible business some place else. What must be done in this case was to nab them both; and not only them, but those in league with them because in a business like this there was a string of villains, evil villains. Yet you could do nothing without proof, could you? And to get proof young girls had first to disappear.

He was running again, although every bone in his body felt tired and all he desired at the moment was to amble or sit down and rest. Yet he felt compelled to run. His feet were stumbling as he negotiated the shallow valley and came within sight of the house. Then his heart seemed to leap into his mouth for there, running towards him, her hair loose in the wind, her skirt billowing around her legs like a balloon, was his granny. Her arms outstretched, she came towards him shouting, but her words were unintelligible until she stood gripping his shoulders and gasping,

'They've gone. Oh! Eddie, they've gone, both of them!'

'No.' The word was just a whimper.

Her head was wagging on her neck now like a golliwog's, the saliva was running from her mouth and the tears were raining down her face. He had never expected to see his granny cry; but it was the very sight of her tears that brought him out of the stupor her words had created, and he yelled now, 'They can't be! Not both of them.' Penny. His first thoughts were for his sister. If anything happened to her his mother would go mad, really mad ... insane ... And he himself would go mad if anything happened to Daisy. Yes he would. In this moment, he knew that he liked Daisy, more than liked her. He had to let his mind say the words: he loved her. Aye, he did. She was his lass; seems she had been, right from the start.

He was running towards the house now, his legs seeming not to be touching the ground, and when he reached the yard he ran in and out of the outbuildings, yelling, 'Penny! Daisy! Penny! Daisy!'

When he eventually stopped in the middle of the yard his granny was facing him, and she said, 'It's no use. It's no use. I've been everywhere and searched every nook and cranny of the house. Penny was with me. I sent her down to ask Daisy to bring up a drink, your grandfather was thirsty. She was a long time in coming back so I went downstairs, and the place was silent. There were three cups and saucers broken on the floor. There must have been more than one of them because one man couldn't have managed two girls, not one like Daisy, who would have fought like a tiger, and apparently did for even the kitchen table was askew. Oh! Eddie, what's come upon us? Did you get Mr Reade?'

'No, granny, he's ... he's gone across the water.'

'Well, go and get the polis, the coastguard, the river polis, anybody.'

'Come on in and sit down.' He thought she was going to collapse and he put his arm around her shoulders and went to lead her towards the kitchen, but she shook off his hold and said, 'Boy! Boy! don't bother with me. Those two children, don't you understand what's going to happen to them? You're not stupid and you're nearing sixteen and a man almost, don't you realize what's going to happen to your sister and that Daisy? Oh my God!' She put her hand over her eyes, and as he stood for a moment watching her he had a great desire to be sick, literally sick. Turning, he fled from her, but when he reached the cliff top he stopped, undecided which way to go, to the right and alert the coastguard or to the left and the river police. But where would he find the river police? It had better be the coastguard, they knew how to go about these things ...

... He was on the point of collapse himself as he reached the coastguard station. There were two men on duty and the elder of the two caught hold of him and said, 'Steady, lad, steady. Now what's your trouble? Your mate fallen over the cliff?'

He began wildly and between gasps,

'Flannagan, I'm Mrs Flannagan's grandson. Me sister and Daisy, Daisy Clinton, the maid, they've been taken, kidnapped.'

'Now! now! now! what's this? Two little girls been kidnapped?'

It was the younger man who cut in on his companion's jocular tone, saying, 'Listen to him. Listen to him, Jimmy.' Then taking Eddie by the shoulder, he shook him gently and said, 'Steady now. Steady. You think two girls have been kidnapped, is that it?'

'Aye, yes, sir.'

'How old are they?'

'Me sister's twelve and Daisy fourteen or so.'

The man now cast a sidelong glance towards his companion; then, his attention on Eddie again, he said, 'Who sent you?'

'Me granny, she's . . . she's nearly mad.'

'Aye, yes, I can understand that.' Again the man looked at his companion and said, 'The captain missing since yesterday, and now the two girls from the house, and Abel Denkin's boat lying off shore. Get word along the coast.' He jerked his head. 'It's a repeat of two years ago but we'll have them this time or die in the attempt.'

The younger man now said briskly, 'And you, me lad, you get to your granny and look after her and tell her to try not to worry. Within a very short time the whole coast will be alerted. By the way, is there anything further you can tell us that might be of use?'

'Yes, yes, I can.' Eddie now nodded at the man. 'It's me granny's nephew who is behind this, Hal

Kemp, and a man called Mr Van, a Belgian man who has been gathering pebbles . . .'

'Jimmy!' The younger man's voice now stopped his companion as he was going out of the door. 'Did you hear that? Now what did I tell you? What have I said all along? I said we should keep an eye on him. Too smooth by half he was; and a man like him spending his time gathering pebbles. The guises those bastards put on to further their business, it makes me blood boil. As for Kemp, I knew he was a petty runner, but we couldn't pin him. Yet I never thought he'd get in this deep. By God! wait till we get them . . . Thanks, boy; now we know who we're after. But go on, do as I tell you, get back home. But keep your eyes open and if anything fresh comes up slip along and let us know.'

As Eddie walked heavily out into the darkening night part of his mind said, Slip along. His feet and legs were so heavy he could hardly lift them, yet his mind was alert, and so full of worry he did not know where to put himself. All he could think of was, Eeh! me mother'll go mad . . . Penny and Daisy. Penny and Daisy.

His grandmother was still outside the house when he returned and he reassured her straightaway, saying, 'The coastguards are going to alert all along the coast. They say not to worry.'

'Oh my God!' His granny closed her eyes for a moment before saying, 'Those are the stupidest words in the English language, not to worry . . . don't worry. I tell you, boy, if those children are not found I'll die, and that is before your mother has the chance to look at me because I couldn't face her. I know how I felt when I lost her but she was still alive, but the best she'll be able to hope for if Penny isn't found is that the child will be lucky and die soon.'

'Oh, granny, shut up! Shut up!' He screwed up his face and bowed his head, and she turned from him and walked towards the house.

After a moment he followed her, and as he entered the kitchen she was going through the far door and he called loudly to her, 'Will I go down to the cove?'

She turned and looked at him and as she shook her head, she said, 'They wouldn't be so stupid as to leave them in the cove because that would be the first place we would think of looking. No, wherever they are they're tied up somewhere waiting to be shipped. They'd have to be taken out to sea from here; they'd never get them across country, not unless they were drugged silly. But . . . but they could be at that.' Her head bobbed with each of the last few words.

And when the door closed on her he sat down on the settle by the side of the fire and, putting his elbows on to his knees, he propped his face in his hands.

He couldn't ever remember crying before and the pain of it now was so intense that he, too, wished he were dead. How was he going to face his mother? How? How? *How*?

His head was brought up by his granny calling his name. Wiping his face with his fingers, he ran from the room and into the hall, there to see her standing at the top of the stairs beckoning to him. 'Come up. Come up a minute. Your granda's fully awake. Come.'

When he reached the bedroom door it was to see her going sideways through the aperture and within seconds he was following her. His grandfather's face looked waxen in the lamplight but his eyes were wide and showed that his mind was clear.

His granny now was talking rapidly, saying, 'Your granda says he found Hal Kemp on Abel Denkin's boat. The Belgian man was there an' all. But all he remembers is that Hal Kemp kept denying that he was up to anything shady and Abel Denkin told him to look around and to take up the hatch and see for himself. And it was as he bent over the hatch that somebody hit him on the head. He doesn't remember anything more except for one thing. As they pretended to lift the hatch he thinks he heard someone bang against it from the inside.'

Eddie looked down at his grandfather, and his grandfather nodded and said slowly, 'I'm . . . I'm sure, boy, there . . . there was somebody in the fish hold, somebody who wanted to get out. They're not very deep the holds, you know. They could have been kneeling or even lying down and thumping upwards with their feet, but they couldn't shout because they were likely gagged. What . . . what you must do is keep an eye on Penny and Daisy because . . . because, boy, that is their business, little girls. I'm certain of it. The swines! The swines!'

Eddie's mouth opened, then closed abruptly when his granny's toe caught him on the leg just above his boot, and he realized that she hadn't told his grandfather of the latest happenings. But now he bent over the old man and said, 'I'll . . . I'll get that news to the coastguards, Granda. They'll . . . they'll know what to do.'

'Aye, lad, you do that and quick, because if I'm not mistaken there's some poor little mite under that hatch and God help her if she's not rescued.' He shook his head now from side to side on the pillow, saying, 'To think in this day and age these things are still allowed to happen.'

'Lie quiet now, Davy, lie quiet. I'll be back in a minute.' She patted his shoulder. Then taking Eddie by the arm, she indicated that he follow her, and when once again they were in the bedroom she looked at him sadly for a moment, saying, 'Boy, I know that you're dead on your feet, but it's essential that the polis or the coastguard know what your granda has just said. And . . . and when Ted comes I'll get him to help me bring your granda into the bedroom.'

'But . . . but how will you explain, Grandma?'

'Leave it to me, boy, I'll think up something. It's unimportant at the moment. What is important . . . well' – she lowered her head – 'you know what is important as well as I do.'

'Yes, Grandma. I'm goin'.'

As he went out of the door she called after him, 'Take something from the pantry and eat it on the way, keep your strength up,' and again he said, 'Yes, Grandma.'

But when he reached the kitchen he didn't go into the pantry, he knew that if he ate a bite it would choke him.

He was leaving the yard when he saw a figure hurrying towards him across the green, and such was his relief that he felt like throwing his arms about Mr Reade.

'What's this now, lad, more trouble?'

'Terrible trouble, Mr Reade, terrible.' He was walking quickly back with Mr Reade towards the kitchen again. 'The two girls, they've gone.'

Ted Reade stopped dead in his tracks. 'What!'

'Aye, aye. If you go upstairs me grandma will tell you all about it, and she wants you to help to get me granda out of the cave room.'

'But . . . but hold your hand a minute, boy.' He caught hold of Eddie's shoulder. 'When did this happen?'

'Late on this afternoon. Me granny twigged what Hal Kemp was up to and she sent me post haste for you and told the girls not to go further than the yard. And when I came back there she was, me granny, on the cliff top like a mad woman. They had both disappeared. But me granda's come to an' he says that Hal Kemp and the Belgian fellow was on Abel Denkin's boat, and that's where he himself was knocked out, and he was sure there was somebody in the hold.'

'God Almighty! what are things comin' to? Well, lad, this is beyond me and what my fellows can do, so you'd better tell the coastguard and the river polis an' all.'

'I've told the coastguard, Mr Reade, and they're telling the polis, but . . . but me granny wants me to let them know about Abel Denkin's boat.'

'Abel Denkin's!' Ted Reade spat out the words.

'By God! I'm tellin' you this, boy, there won't be much left of Abel Denkin and your Mr Hal Kemp if my fellows an' the fishermen lay their hands on them afore the polis or the coastguards. I'm tellin' you there won't be much of them left. Smugglin' is one thing but white slavery with bairns is another. Aye, by God! it is that. But go on, lad; take to your heels.'

Eddie took to his heels, but just at a trot, carrying a lantern now. He made for the coastguard station again.

On reaching it he found a different man on duty but he seemed conversant with all that had happened, and when Eddie told him about Abel Denkin's boat the man said, 'Good, good. And you say your grandfather is back? How did that come about?'

'I . . . I don't know.' Eddie stammered, 'I just got in and . . . and there he was, and me granny sent me post haste . . . back here.'

'What a business! What a business! It's going to be a long night for everybody. Go on back home, lad, and try not to worry. If it's humanly possible the bairns will be found.'

Try not to worry! As his granny said, those were the silliest words in the language when put together like that. The fact is one should worry until the thing that was causing the worry was solved, 'cos if you didn't worry you would do nothing about it, would you?

When he reached the house again there were two strange men in the kitchen, one in plain clothes and one in uniform. His granny, who had been talking to them, turned as he entered the room and said, 'This is me grandson,' and he warmed to her for a moment as she added, 'He's never been off his feet since last night, he's dead beat.'

The man in plain clothes nodded towards him and said, 'Hello there. Nasty business this, nasty business. Your grandmother has told us all she knows but if you don't mind I would like you to go over it from the beginning, right back from when you first saw Mr Kemp and his Belgian friend together.' The man now pulled a chair out for him and as he sat down he was aware that perhaps for the first time in his life he wasn't being treated as a boy, and so it wasn't in the faltering tones of a boy that he repeated all he knew about Hal Kemp and his foreign friend.

It was about fifteen minutes later when the visitors were about to take their leave that his granny asked them, 'Are you away now to search the boat, Denkin's boat, that's lying out there?'

When neither of the men replied for a moment but exchanged glances his granny cried in her old raucous fashion, 'Why in the name of God are you hesitating? You heard what I told you, what my husband said, there's somebody on there already if my two haven't joined them?'

'Mrs Flannagan –' The plain clothes man put his hand on her arm and said softly, 'In a game like this, a serious game like this, you cannot accuse anybody on hearsay, you've got to catch them with the goods on them, so to speak. If there was anybody on that boat yesterday it's not likely they're still there; and it's not likely either that your grandchild or your little maid has been taken aboard, not yet anyway. The boat, to all intents and purposes, is lying off there waiting for high tide; that it's not lying at the quay with the others is neither here nor there; there's no law against its anchoring out a bit, and they could always say they were doing a bit of inshore fishing. What we reckon is that they have arranged a time for picking up their cargo and . . . well, it'll be up to us to stop them loading it. But on no account do we want them to be forearmed.'

Eddie watched his grandmother nod slowly as she said, 'Well, there might be something in that, but do you realize that I'm nearly beside meself with worry?'

'We realize that, Mrs Flannagan.'

As the plain clothes man spoke, the constable who was standing slightly behind Mrs Flannagan now signalled to Eddie that he should go outside, and so after a moment he rose and, picking up the lighted lantern that he had set on the lamp rack near the kitchen door, he said, 'I'll show you down the yard.'

'That's good of you, boy,' the plain clothes man said; 'two lanterns are better than one . . . Good-night, Mrs Flannagan.'

'Good night. And you'll let me know as soon as you hear anything?'

'The moment we hear anything at all we'll send someone along. Good-night.'

Out in the yard it was the policeman who now said, 'It's no use worrying her more than is necessary, but you yourself, lad, will have guessed by now that we're not dealing with a gang of young 'uns who are playing at pirates, and nobody but a fool would leave a boat out there for the river polis to trip over, now would they? They must know by now that the whole coast is alerted. How we look at it' – he turned and indicated the plain clothes man – 'is that Abel Denkin's boat is simply a decoy; while we're waiting for them to load their precious cargo it will be in the process of being trundled off to another part of the coast where likely another boat is lying in wait. So it's up to us to find this particular boat. But we can't do much till daylight, you understand?'

Aye, he understood; and at the same time he saw that he had been gullible. Of course, it was as the river police said, men in a game like this were no amateurs.

The thought made him feel sick again. His voice was thick and cracked now as he asked, 'Do . . . do you think you'll be able to find them?'

'Well, it won't be for want of tryin'; and although we can't do much on the water until dawn we intend to search the whole shore; there's caves and nooks and crannies along the whole stretch that they just might be using. On the other hand, what we must also take into consideration is that they may not ship them at all for weeks but keep them hidden somewhere. There's always those who'll do anything for money, and the most unsuspected houses could be acting as prisons. It's been known to happen.'

Eddie stared dumbly at the man; the new aspect he was putting on the situation appeared more terrifying.

The plain clothes man now said, 'Go on and

stay with your grandmother. By the way, has she no relatives that she could call on at such a time as this? She needs someone in the house anyway to help nurse the captain.'

'No, no, there's only my mother and . . . and she's away in hospital. She's not well.'

'Oh! That's a pity. Well, good-night, boy. We'll be seeing you soon.'

'Good-night, sir.' He turned and went back into the kitchen, and as he did so he thought, Yes, this was the time his granny did need some help, some woman . . . perhaps Biddy. Biddy would be back from her Sunday jaunt across the water now. He'd go down for her.

He said this immediately. 'Granny, I'll go down and tell Biddy to come up, eh?'

Mrs Flannagan looked at him for a moment, then moved her head slowly as she said, 'I'd thought of that but I didn't want to put you to another trail.' Then her head slightly to the side, she said, 'Why did you go out with the men? Did they want to tell you something? Nothing much escapes me you know, boy; that bit about the lantern wouldn't have deceived a child. They came with one lantern they could go back with one lantern. And they say the men only get into the river polis if they've got cats' eyes.'

He hung his head for a moment, but presently said, 'They think there may be another boat lying along the coast somewhere and they're just using Denkin's as a blind.'

He watched her bite on her lower lip. 'Aye, yes, that's possible,' she said. 'And it wouldn't have worried me anymore if they had told me, it would only have proved that they have got their heads screwed on the right way and they're up to all the tricks of that evil lot. Anyway, sit down here and have this bite to eat, then you can do as you said and go along to Biddy's.' She shook her head now. 'It's funny, I've known Biddy McMann all my life – she came here to work when she was eight years old and I was but three – but I've never known her to be in the right place at the right time yet; she's never there when she's wanted. It wouldn't surprise me when you got there to find the place in darkness because she's spending the night over the water with that no good son of hers who'll neither work nor want.'

Half an hour later when Eddie was swinging the lantern before the darkened windows of the cottage he thought, and not for the first time, Me Granny's a witch.

He was tired, he was weary and worried sick, but as he returned along the coast road, one small spark of comfort was given him as he saw the pin points of light from the lanterns stretching away along the shore. As the river police had said, they were leaving no stone unturned.

7

Eddie slowly opened his eyes. When he tried to lift his head he groaned aloud; he had been sleeping in the armchair to the side of his grandfather's bed. He had a crick in his neck; and as he moved his head from side to side he looked across to where his grandmother was sitting in the other chair and he saw what he imagined had woken him up. She was slapping the side of her face vigorously with her hand and talking away to herself, making use of a number of small oaths. 'Damn you! Damn the thing! Nerve complaint. Come and go, they said.' Slap! Slap! Slap!

'You would play up at this time, wouldn't you? Don't tell me I've got to wear that blasted trumpet again, and for real now.' Slap! Slap! Slap! 'Aw.' She became aware that Eddie had woken up. Pointing to her ear, she said, 'It's acting the goat. Couldn't hear a thing.'

He rose unsteadily to his feet and, going towards her, he said, 'Don't worry.' Those silly words again; he was as bad as the rest. Then turning and going to the side table, he picked up the trumpet and brought it to her and, putting it to her ear, said, 'It'll come back when this is over.'

'What!' She turned her screwed-up face toward him.

He shouted now, 'It'll come back, your hearin' 'll come back once all this business is over. It's because you're worrying that you've lost it.'

She took the trumpet from his hand and there was a pitiable look on her face as she said, 'You were shouting I know and I could hardly hear you, but as you say once me mind's at rest . . . aw, dear God, haven't I enough to put up with!' She now looked towards the clock. 'Five o'clock. I'll go down and make a pot of tea.'

'No, you stay where you are, I'll see to it.' He was shouting into the trumpet again.

She made no protest but nodded at him now, saying, 'Half sleep is worse than no sleep at all I think; you don't know if you're dreaming or still awake.'

As he reached the door, he stopped. Her words had stirred something in his mind. It wasn't her slapping her ear that had woken him, but a dream, like that dream that he'd had the other night. He had seen that man again, the one in the peak cap and the reefer jacket, the young man with the jolly face. And . . . and what had he done?

He turned now and looked towards the side of the bed where the door led into the cave room. The man had taken him through there, he had taken him by the hand and pulled him down the steps, down the slopes. He remembered now that he had pulled him so quickly that his feet hadn't touched the ground at all. Then when they got to

137

the place where the loop was and the two planks over the crevasse, he had disappeared; like a flash of lightning he had disappeared. But he himself had gone bounding on down the slope and into the candle room. And there he had opened the door that led into the cave, and it was the thunder of the waves dashing against the rocks that had woken him up.

'What is it? Why are you looking like that?' His granny was coming towards him.

He shook his head, then mouthed, 'I . . . I had a funny dream.'

'What?'

When he went to mouth the words again, she said, 'Oh, blast!' and, going quickly back to the table, she picked up the trumpet, put the cord round her head as if in resignation, and held the horn to her ear, and he shouted into it, 'I had a strange dream. I . . . I was remembering it.'

She looked at him. 'What kind of a dream?'

Again he was shouting into the trumpet, but as he did so he looked towards the bed in case he should wake his grandfather, but the old man was deep in sleep as his snores proclaimed, and so he said, 'I've . . . I've had it afore. A man in a peak cap, like . . . like a sailor fellow. He came and took me through the door there.' He pointed towards the head of the bed. 'He dragged me through, pushing and pulling me down the steps. I sort of knew he was leading me to the cave, but when we came to the loop where the crevasse is he disappeared and, well, I seemed to go on, and when I opened the door the noise of the waves inside the cave woke me up.'

He watched his granny slowly take the trumpet from her ear and stare hard at him for a moment before turning and looking towards the head of the bed, and her mouth was open when she looked at him again and she said, 'You say he pulled you through there?'

He nodded at her now, and he watched her head going back on her shoulder and her eyes move round the room as if she was looking for somebody floating in the air. When she brought her gaze back to him she said, 'Uncle Dan.' Then again, 'Uncle Dan.' And now her voice a whisper, she added, 'Dear God! Dear God! it just could be. It's just as me father described him ... Come back.' She now dragged him back from the door, shot the bolt in it; then hurrying across the room, she said, 'Light the candles.'

While, with shaking hands, he lit the two candles that were standing in brass candlesticks on the side table, he watched her hurry into the cupboard. Then, his amazement as fresh as it had been when he first witnessed the wall moving inwards, he went to step through the aperture but paused as his granny, bending over the bed, touched her husband's face, then muttered, 'He's all right; he'll sleep for hours. Go on. Go on.' She was pushing him in her impetuous way now into the wall room. But when they stood above the stairway she grabbed a candlestick from him and preceded him down the steps.

It was as he went down the slope clinging on to the rope balustrade that the fear returned to him again, and he questioned why his approach to that one spot in this whole eerie passageway should create such a feeling in him. He had only been past it twice but it seemed to him as if he had known the place all his life. He tried to analyse his fear. Was it because the place seemed evil? No ... no, he couldn't say it gave him the impression of being evil or horrifying. Well then what was creating this feeling? The terrible noise that came from the depth of the hole or just the hole itself?

No. Again, no.

Then what?

When the word came to him, he literally shook his head at it. *Sadness. No.* But yes, that was the feeling that contributed mostly to his fear, a feeling of great sadness of some tragedy past, or yet to come, a loss, an emptiness ...

'Now watch your feet, lad, we're coming to the loop.'

He knew they were coming to the loop; there was the roar getting louder and louder in his ears, deafening now as he pressed his side against the wall and tried to avert his gaze from the two planks of wood that lay across the void to the left of him ...

They were round it now and going down the slope.

Then they were in the candle room and Eddie was applying all his strength to the lever, but without much avail.

'Here! let me help.' His granny had to reach up on her toes in order to grip the handle, but her added weight did the trick and now the lever slowly moved downwards and there was the grinding sound as if stones were being crushed as the rock door swung slowly open and let in the roar of the sea.

Now he was hanging out through the aperture looking down into the dimly lit cave and in utter amazement on to a face staring up at him, a black face in which the eyes looked enormous, the face of a trussed-up black boy. The trousered legs were bound, as were the wrists. The boy was lying on his side with his head turned towards them; his mouth was open and from it was protruding a piece of rag. He had a cap on his head which he seemed to be trying to dislodge now by rubbing the side of his head against the sand.

'It's a lad!' Eddie yelled at his granny, who was kneeling by his side. Then springing to his feet, he grabbed the rope ladder from the wall and, pushing his granny aside, he clipped the hooks into the staples at each side of the wall below the door as he had seen her do, then threw the ladder out and into the cave. Within seconds he was scrambling down it.

When he knelt by the boy's side and looked down into his eyes his heart seemed to leap into his mouth with shock. The next minute he was tearing the gag from the boy's mouth and pulling off his cap at the same time.

'Aw, Ed . . . die. Ed . . . die!'

'It's Daisy! It's Daisy!' He was yelling up to his granny now, and Mrs Flannagan's head was bobbing as if on wires.

'Aw, Eddie! I . . . I thought I was a gonner. Aw, Eddie!' Daisy's voice broke into a wail as she burst out crying.

He had loosened her wrists and was undoing

141

the last knot in the rope that tied her ankles when the dim light in the cave was made dimmer still by a figure blocking the entrance.

As Daisy and Mrs Flannagan yelled simultaneously, 'Eddie! Eddie! look out!' Hal Kemp sprang over the cave floor, paused for a second only as he gazed in sheer astonishment at his aunt's head and shoulders hanging out from a hole in the rock above his head; then with a snort of rage he was on Eddie.

Against the bulk of the man Eddie's youthful strength would have had as much effect as that of an amateur against a trained boxer, but in this instance Eddie was fortified with a rage that made him momentarily equal to the man, for now he was flaying into him with his fists and his feet, and instead of Hal Kemp being able to fell him to the ground with one blow he found he was having to defend himself; and this he did, smashing his fists first in the direction of Eddie's face, then into his body, which blows Eddie fortunately managed to ward off, coming back with some effectual punches of his own. But it was when Hal Kemp's right hand caught him full in the mouth and his left hand swinging downwards lashed into his stomach that the breath left his body and his feet left the ground, and he writhed in agony on the rock floor. And that likely would have been the end of him, but as Hal Kemp's boot came backwards to deliver a kick at him, Daisy, grabbing at his hand, set her teeth into it. With a yell he rounded on her, and his raised fist was about to descend on her when he suddenly stopped and his whole body became momentarily still in a pose from which it is certain he would have recovered almost immediately had not Mrs Flannagan, from where she was positioned half-way down the ladder, brought her ear trumpet down fully on his head for a second time. When his body swayed she completed her attack by swinging her arm wide and delivering the third blow just below the ear. And on this, it was as if he had been felled by an ox, for, sinking to the floor, he lay there in a crumpled heap.

'Come on, boy! On your feet. Get up! Get up!'

Eddie drew in a number of deep gasping breaths before he could turn on to his knees, and then, his granny at one side of him and Daisy at the other, they led him to the foot of the ladder. There his granny's voice spurred him up as she cried, 'Get up, boy! And you, too, Daisy. Up you go!'

Obediently now, Eddie climbed the ladder but when he reached the candle room he again col-lapsed on the floor. His face seemed to be swell-ing to twice its size, his mouth felt numb and he could taste blood. There was something on his tongue, and when he spat it out it made a pinging sound as it hit the rock wall. He had lost a tooth.

But where was his granny? He crawled now to the aperture to see Mrs Flannagan standing in the opening of the cave looking towards the sea, and he called weakly to her, 'Gran! Gran! come on.' But knowing she couldn't hear him, he willed her to turn and after a moment she did and moved quickly towards the ladder. When he had helped her through the aperture she quickly rose from her knees and, going to the lever, closed the door. Not until then did she turn to Daisy and voice the thought that was raging through Eddie's head. 'Where's Penny? What's happened to Penny?'

Looking from one to the other, Daisy shook her head and, the tears running down her face, she whimpered, 'They . . . they took her along the coast, I think, to . . . to another boat. She cried a lot and they made her drink something.'

'Speak up! Speak up!' Mrs Flannagan pressed the dented trumpet closer to her ear. Then after Daisy repeated what she had already said, Mrs Flannagan exclaimed, 'Oh dear Lord! Dear Lord! . . . was she dressed like this?' She touched the sleeve of the boy's jacket that Daisy was wearing, and Daisy nodded, saying, 'Aye. And there were another two lasses; they were all dressed as boys. Oh, it was dreadful, it was awful.' Her head swung from side to side now, and again she was crying aloud.

'It's all right. It's all right.' Mrs Flannagan had her arms about her. 'You're safe now. Don't cry, but try to think. Tell us everything you heard.'

Daisy now gulped in her throat and wiped her black smeared face on the back of her hand; then speaking into the horn again, she said, 'They're goin' in a boat called, I think it's Lar Sea Queen or some word like that. It appears from what Mr Hal said . . . Eeh! I hate to think of him as Mr Hal.'

'Go on, never mind about that. What did he say?'

'Well, he was talkin' to that Mr Van. Oh, if ever

anybody was taken in in their life, missis, it was me by that man.'

'Daisy!'

'Aye. Well, missis, Hal Kemp had already taken two lasses along in the cart during the night, but he had to bring them back 'cos he couldn't get them on board or something and they kept them for most of the time in the hold of some ship, and then early on this morning that Mr Van said they'd split up, something about a half a loaf better than no bread. I think he was meaning if one boat was caught the other could get away. It was Mr Denkin's boat they put some of us on. It seemed that things hadn't gone right somewhere and they had to use it for some of us. But there was one lass there, she said she didn't mind, and so they didn't tie her up or anything. She said anything was better than standin' in a pie and pea shop fourteen hours a day for half-a-crown a week. And . . . and that Mr Van, he got her to talk to me, an' he tried to get round me. He kept saying that if I'd been a sensible girl I would have enjoyed meself sailing on the boat and having nice food and all that.

'You . . . you know what I did?' She appealed now first to one and then to the other, and when both Mrs Flannagan and Eddie remained silent, she said, 'I tore at his face with me nails and . . . and you know what he did then?'

Again they remained silent, and now her head drooped and she said, 'It . . . it was frightenin', more than if he had lashed out at me; he smiled and then he laughed, and then he said he liked them with spunk and I would have plenty of opportunity to scratch and tear where I was going. Aw, missis, I was scared, I was scared silly.' Daisy now fell against Mrs Flannagan and again the old woman's arms went about her and her voice was tender as she said, 'Come on. Come on; let us get out of this. Now' – she pulled Daisy to her feet – 'I'm going on ahead and you do exactly what Eddie tells you. Don't put a step wrong. And when you get back into the house I want you to forget all about how you got there; I want you to tell the polis that we came on you by the beach way. You understand?'

Daisy paused, then glanced around the candle room as if its strangeness was only now registering with her; then she whispered, 'Aye, aye, missis.'

As he now gripped Daisy's hand and guided her up the incline, Eddie thought it wasn't much use his granny trying to keep the whereabouts of the passage a secret, for Hal Kemp would open his mouth wide if he was caught by the police; and if he wasn't he could still find a way of informing other cronies, and then whatever reason his granny had for keeping the presence of the passage secret would be brought into the open.

The policemen were in the kitchen, four of them, all of different ranks, and Daisy, looking from one to the other from where she sat by the fire, washed now and in her usual clothes, wished they would stop asking her the same thing over and over again. She had told them exactly what the missis had told her to say, and that was that

146

Eddie had found her tied up in one of the shallow caves. Two men had brought her in the cart to the top of the cliff, then had carried her down, and they seemed to be expecting a boat. When it didn't come they pushed her into the far corner of the cave and warned her to be quiet. But she couldn't be anything else, because she had the rag in her mouth. Then Eddie had come along and rescued her and they had got up the cliff path by the broken steps. But what the police kept on about was the name of the ship, and for what seemed to her the thousandth time, she said, 'I can't think of anything more, I've told you everything.'

'Well, just think, just once more.' The tall officer was bending down to her. 'Are you sure the name of the boat was The Sea Queen?'

'Aye, I heard it three or four times.'

The men now looked at each other; they looked at Mrs Flannagan and they looked at Eddie; then the tall man said, 'We've telegraphed to Sunderland and as far as Grimsby and there's no boat registered there under that name.'

'Sir.' They all turned and looked in Eddie's direction now, and he swallowed before he said, 'When Daisy first mentioned hearin' the name of the boat she said Lar Sea Queen not The Sea Queen.'

'Did I?' Daisy was staring at him, and he nodded towards her, saying, 'Aye, that's what you said the first time, Lar Sea Queen.'

'*Lar Sea Queen. Lar Sea Queen.* We're fools, it's Le Sequin!' One of the four was shouting excitely now.

'It was on the register we went through this morning. Le Sequin: port of registry, Brussels. Come on. Come on!' The man made hastily for the door, then turned back again and, reaching out his arm, patted Eddie on the shoulder, saying, 'Good boy. Good boy.'

They were all gone and the kitchen seemed strangely quiet until Mrs Flannagan joined her hands together and, bowing her head towards them, muttered, 'Dear God! Dear God! have mercy on those poor children and grant that the authorities will get there afore the ship sails. And . . . and bring my Penelope safely back.'

The minutes seemed to pass like hours and the hours seemed as long as days. Eddie had lost count of the times that he had gone at his granny's bidding on to the cliff path to see if there was any sign of the coastguard or the policemen returning, and it was around noon when he yet again walked over the wet grass towards the cliff path.

He was sick with worry over Penny's fate and the effect her disappearance would have on his mother when she found out. And as his granny had just said, she would know at least by tomorrow for the papers would be full of it tonight. Oh, how he wished his mother had taken his advice and let them stay at home, because the very thing she had feared had come about, and because of this she would blame herself more than ever.

If only he could do something. But both his granny and Daisy would hardly let him out of their sight. He had suggested that he go into the town and get news at first hand, but his granny had said, 'No, stay here, lad.' As for Daisy she had stood so close to him, like a bairn seeking protection, that he had felt embarrassed.

As he reached a point on the path where he could see for some distance along the cliff path his heartbeat quickened as he saw a number of men coming towards him. Two were pushing and two were pulling a long handle flat cart. As they came nearer he recognized one of the men as the coastguard he had spoken to yesterday. Then his whole body gave a jerk as he saw what they were hauling on the cart. It was a man.

They stopped as they came abreast of him. But the men didn't speak to him, nor he to them, for almost a minute as he stood gazing down on the dead face of Hal Kemp.

'He's . . . he's . . . ?'

'Aye, lad, he's dead. And perhaps it's just as well for him as things have turned out.'

'Where . . . where did you find him?'

'In the mouth of the cave down there. We saw him bobbing about some time ago but couldn't do much until the tide was on the turn. We got him just before it took him out.'

Eddie swallowed deeply. The blows his granny had levelled at him must have stunned him, and then the tide came in. But . . . but what about the other man in the boat? His granny had glimpsed that there was another man waiting off shore in the sculler. Why hadn't he come back for him? The only explanation he could give himself was that the man hearing the commotion in the cave must have thought it was a police trap, or some such, and had gone off, leaving his accomplice to his fate. But what would his granny say? How would she take it when she knew that the blows she had rained on her nephew with her trumpet had so knocked him out that he hadn't recovered? And yet the trumpet wasn't all that heavy. But heavy or not she must have brought it down with some force, and on a vital spot.

'Where . . . where are you takin' him?'

'That's the point, lad. Don't know whether we should take him to the house' – the man made a motion with his head – 'or go on to the mortuary.'

'I . . . I would go on if I were you. Me granny's been through a lot these last few days and she's worried sick about me sister. I . . . I don't think she could stand anymore, not at present.'

'You're right, lad, you're right. Anyway, under the circumstances I don't suppose he'd be welcome in her house again, dead or alive.'

'No, you're right there.'

As he watched the men moving away along the cliff path he felt no tinge of remorse that Hal Kemp was dead. As the man had said, it was likely all for the best because if he had been caught he would have rotted in prison for years, and likely gone through hell there from other prisoners, for even the worst of wrongdoers hated men who in any way harmed children.

Now he had the task of breaking the news to his granny.

A few minutes later he was standing in the kitchen and finding it difficult to know where to start. He stood staring at her until she cried at

150

him, 'What is it? What have you heard? Tell me, boy, what have you heard?'

She now put the trumpet, the mouthpiece which was no longer round but had one side dented almost to the middle, to her ear and Eddie cried into it, 'It's all right; it isn't news of Penny. It's . . . it's Hal Kemp.'

The ear trumpet was whisked away. and Mrs Flannagan now demanded, 'What about him?'

'He's dead.'

She read his lips and her mouth opened slightly and she repeated, 'Dead?' and he nodded once.

'How?'

He swallowed twice before he said, 'Drowned.'

'What?'

He was again speaking into the trumpet. 'He was drowned.'

They stared at each other until she said, 'That fellow in the boat, he mustn't have come back then?'

He shook his head.

'I must have knocked him out.'

Slowly now he put the trumpet to her ear and said, 'Well, if you hadn't, I know one thing, you would have been two grandchildren short at this minute because he meant to do for me. I could see it in his face.'

Again they were looking at each other, and now, her head nodding slightly, she said, 'Yes, you're right there.' Then she jerked her chin upwards as she exclaimed, 'Oh, don't worry, boy, don't you worry, me conscience isn't going to trouble me on that account. Oh no. The only thing I'm thinking at this moment is, it was too easy a death for him. By! aye, it was that. And I hope the other gentleman doesn't escape so easily; I want to see justice take its course there, and a long course at that. And all those in league with him . . .' Her head was wagging on her shoulders as she ended, 'I'll go up now and tell your grandfather, and if I know him he'll want to pin a medal on me for getting rid of the scum.'

Both Eddie and Daisy watched her turn around and march up the kitchen and out through the door and Daisy, her voice holding a tone of awe, whispered, 'She's marvellous, isn't she. Wonderful!'

Marvellous! Wonderful! He wouldn't have used those terms in connection with his granny. Tough is the word he would have used, real tough. She wasn't womanly at all; although he had seen her soften once or twice of late, her reactions to most things were more like those of a man.

'Would you get me a bucket of coal in, Eddie?'

He turned and looked at Daisy. She had never before asked him to do anything for her. 'Aye. Yes.' He went and picked up the brass scuttle that was standing to the side of the hearth, and when he passed her she said, 'I'm . . . I'm afraid to go into the backyard.'

'But it's all right now.'

She shook her head at this, then pressed her fingers over her lips before saying, 'No, no; it won't be all right for me until they get him, that Mr Van. He's clever. Aye, an' wily. That Hal Kemp was bad in one way but . . . but that Mr Van, I know now he's like the devil 'cos he could smile an' be pleasant when he was doing awful things. No' – she shook her head – 'I'll be frightened to put me foot across the door until they get him.'

He didn't now say, 'Oh, don't be silly,' because he knew that in her place he would be feeling the same.

He went out and filled the scuttle, and as he was returning across the yard two men entered it. He put the scuttle down on the ground and stood waiting, and when they neared him one of the men just shook his head, and Eddie, stooping, lifted the scuttle and went into the kitchen. They followed him.

'Will you sit down a minute?' He turned from them to Daisy, saying now, 'Go and tell me granny the polis are here.'

'You didn't find the boat then?' He was looking from one to the other of the men.

'Yes, lad, we found the boat all right and we rescued four bairns. And there's a number of men behind bars in the Sunderland Jail at this minute, but I'm afraid your sister wasn't one of the children.'

He turned from them and put his hand to his throat as if to loosen the tension, then as the kitchen door opened to admit his granny he went out into the yard again because he couldn't bear to witness her reaction to the news.

It was when he had been standing in the dark quietness of the stable for about ten minutes that Eddie asked himself a question, and he wondered why he hadn't asked it before. The question was:

153

What had become of Barney and the cart? He remembered his grandfather saying that the horse must have been used for night work because it appeared so worn out. He also knew that although both the cart and horse were supposed to belong to Hal Kemp, it was his grandmother who had set him up with it to start a little business of fish transporting from the quay to the shops. But where were the cart and horse now?

Perhaps somewhere in Sunderland.

It was evident that they had used it as a means of transport for what they termed their cargo. But if it had been left on the Shields quay the police would have spoken about it before now.

Where else, he now asked himself, could they have hidden a horse and cart along this stretch? It wasn't likely they had taken it down to the beach and hidden it in one of the shallow caves, because Barney liked company and he would have set up a neighing. Nor was it likely that Hal Kemp would have paid a hostler to see to the animal. So where could the horse and cart be?

... He was on his feet when the probable answer came to him. Biddy McMann's ... Biddy had a shed outside her cottage. It was a good size, not quite as big as the barn here, but it would take a cart and horse all right. And hadn't the gentleman, Mr Van, lodged with Biddy until he disappeared? And who would think of looking for him in his old lodgings, for no man would be mad enough or ... *clever enough* to hide out under the police force's nose, so to speak.

He had passed the end of the yard and was

speeding over the grass when he heard one of the men hailing him from the house, but he took no notice. His legs seeming to have acquired a separate strength of their own, he leapt over mounds and rough ground, down the shallow valley, up the other side and for some way along the cliff top before he turned inland. And he was still running when, like a speck in a field, he saw Biddy's cottage.

He was within a hundred feet of it when he drew to a halt and stared at it. The cottage was a small place, consisting of only two rooms up and two rooms down with a lean-to at the back that Biddy used as a scullery.

The door of the cottage was closed but that was no indication that she was out.

He kept his steps slow and trod lightly as he neared the door and turned the handle. It was locked. He now moved cautiously along the wall to where the single window was draped with lace curtains. Dropping on to his hunkers he looked through the clear space left by the curtains where they were parted and gathered into a loop at each side of the window. The room was empty and the fire was out. Definitely Biddy hadn't returned from . . . across the water. It was as his granny said, she was never there when she was wanted. He could imagine her coming jauntily into the house tomorrow and saying, 'Well now, Maggie, if I'd only known you were in need of me I would have been here like a shot. Now you know I would.'

He moved past the window but didn't go round to the back of the cottage; instead, he made his way to the outbuildings that stood facing him. Gently he lifted the latch of the door and as gently pushed it wide but didn't enter. He didn't want a blow on the head from the side. The place was lighted only by the daylight coming through the cracks made by the warped wood, but it was like a note of welcome being given to him when he heard the horse neigh.

His eyes darting here and there, he went slowly forward until he reached the horse; then stroking its muzzle, he said softly, 'Hello, Barney old boy. Hello there,' and the horse tossed its head and neighed again.

'All right. All right. Quiet. I'll be back in a minute.'

He patted the animal's flank, then went quickly out and across the narrow yard and to the door leading into the lean-to.

The door, as he expected, was locked but the make-shift window to the right of it had an ordinary sneck latch which could be moved by inserting a thin blade between the upper and lower sections. He had got in through the back window of their own house more than once in this way; once when his mother had lost her key and another time when he came home from work in the middle of the day with a burnt finger and his mother was out.

But where would he find a thin blade now? He didn't carry a knife, having always resisted the temptation after seeing what could happen when tempers got out of hand and pocket knives were brought in to enforce an argument.

He looked about him. There was a poss tub and

a wooden roller mangle to the side of the lean-to, and on the draining board of the mangle was a handleless broken-bladed knife, used, he saw, for cutting up soap, blue mottled soap, for the prong which had once been inserted into a bone handle gave evidence of this with the pieces of dry soap adhering to it.

He wondered as he picked up the knife why Biddy didn't keep her mangle and her poss tub in the shed. Likely because it was too far away from her source of hot water.

The knife did its work, and quietly he pushed up the bottom half of the small window. But even as he crawled through and fell onto his hands on the stone floor he asked himself what he expected to find, and grimly the answer came from deep within him, 'We'll see, won't we? We'll see. If I'm wrong, well, I'm wrong, but if I'm right . . .!'

The door from the lean-to led straight into the kitchen-cum-living room and right opposite was the front door, but to the left of him was a door leading into the other room, the room Biddy always referred to as 'me parlour'.

Even as he tip-toed towards it he knew that if there was anyone in the house they would already be aware of his presence, the neighing of the horse alone would alert them, so deciding to use surprise tactics he took his foot and thrust it against the parlour door. It opened easily and when it reached its full extent it hit some object behind it which thrust it closed again. But he had seen enough of the room to know that it was empty, unless . . . unless there was someone behind the door.

He now opened the door slightly and peered through the aperture between the door and its stanchion. It gave him a clear view of that part of the room, and there was no one in it.

He turned now and looked towards where the stairs led upwards to the right of the door which gave onto the scullery. When he reached the foot of them he stared into the dark abyss they presented. If anybody was up there they were waiting for him and they had all the advantages.

He stood for a full minute considering. Having made up his mind he made no bones about being quiet, but walked across the room towards the front door, then walked back to the kitchen door and out into the lean-to. There he withdrew the bolt from the outer door, then banged it closed again, and now, stooping down, he quickly undid the laces of his boots and pulled them off.

He was again standing at the bottom of the stairs when he heard a door open above him. Pressing himself against the side of the wall now, he waited for someone to descend.

When he heard no further movement at all on the stairs or from up above, he reckoned that whoever was up there must have surmised that he had left, that is if they had been in the front upper room of the cottage; if they had been in the back room all they needed to have done was to look out of the window and they would have known immediately that he hadn't left.

The minutes passed and still there was no sound from up above; so now he pressed himself from the wall and began to ascend the stairs, cautiously placing each foot on the side of the treads in the hope that they wouldn't creak.

The stairs were dark right to the top but there was sufficient light on the tiny landing given off by a fanlight in the roof for him to make out that both bedroom doors were closed.

He surmised that his quarry would be in the front room and so it was this door that he pounced on and burst open. Immediately he saw his mistake for the room was empty. He swung round and faced the other door and although his body was taut he was trembling now in every limb; it was as if all his bones were attached to wires.

He waited, staring unblinking towards the closed door. Had he imagined he'd heard a door open and close? Had he come on a wild goose chase? No, no; some instinct told him he hadn't and it was this same instinct that made him bend forward, lift the latch of the door with one hand while with his foot he kicked it open . . .

Now he stood staring wide-eyed into the small room for straight before him was a bed and lying on it was Penny, apparently sound asleep, and standing at the head of the bed was *the man, the Belgian, the stone gatherer, the child gatherer*.

It was the man who spoke first. 'It has taken you some time to make the stairs,' he said. There was no smile on his face now, yet the voice was still smooth, the words broken slightly with the foreign accent.

Eddie made no reply but slowly lifted one foot forward, then the other. The third step brought him to the foot of the bed, and here he gripped hold of the brass rail. His mind was giving him words to speak such as 'You filthy swine! You dirty rotten swine! I'm going to kill you. Do you know I'm going to kill you?' But he couldn't get them past his lips because his jaws wouldn't work, they were so tightly clenched.

When he sprang it was to meet the man's forearm across his chest, and the blow sent him reeling back to the wall. But the impact with the wall seemed to help him to spring forward again, and now he was grappling with the hated individual. They were on the floor rolling in the confined space between the wall and the bed. At one point he was uppermost with the man's neck between his hands, then the man's knee came up sharply to his groin. He gasped and rolled aside. This was the same trick that had disabled him in the cave. But now his fury was so great that it did nothing more than make him gasp before his hands went out again to combat the blows that the man was now raining on him.

Again they were rolling on the floor, and again he was uppermost and somewhere inside his raging brain he knew he was getting the upper hand and that the man was weakening, and when he heard him gasp, 'Enough! Enough! Let . . . let me go. You . . . you have won,' he still went on pounding him until he told himself that should he succeed in killing him the man would escape justice, the justice that years of imprisonment would mete out.

Sanity returning to him, his arms dropped to his sides and he stumbled to his feet and, backing away towards the foot of the bed, he gasped, 'Get up!'

For a time the man seemed unable to move, and when he did it was to turn on his hands and knees and crawl a few paces to where a small open valise lay on the floor.

Eddie watched him clutching at the scattered clothes as if for support; he watched him pull himself to his feet by the help of a wooden chair; and so when the seemingly defeated man sprang on him he was completely off his guard.

At first he thought the man had stuck a hot poker in his shoulder, and when he dropped onto the foot of the bed gasping and saw the knife come up again he put out his hands to save himself. As the blood from his hands spurted into his eyes and he fell backwards across the bed he knew that the man's knife had found another place in his body and that this was the end of him. All his effort had been in vain, and Penny, across whose feet he was lying, would be taken away and his granny would die . . . and his mother would go mad.

There was a great roaring in his head, a great confusion; he was in the cave once more fighting Hal Kemp. No, no, he wasn't, he was standing near the hole and the man with the peak cap was dancing round it. He was doing an Irish jig like Biddy McMann did when she had had a drop. The blood was in his mouth, it was choking him. Oh Ma! Ma! Oh Ma! If she only hadn't gone away. If she'd only let him stay at home. He was going down, down, down the hole in the passage; but he wasn't bumping himself for the man in the peak cap had his arms about him.

8

If only that fellow in the peak cap would stay in one place and he would stop bringing people into the room. One minute he was chasing him along the passage and scaring the wits out of him as he jumped over the hole, then the next minute he was running across the grass towards him holding his mother by one hand and Penny with the other; and he never seemed to do anything slowly or quietly like other people.

Two doctors at one go he brought in, that old Doctor Collington and a younger man, and between them they put him through it. By lad! they did. Stuck needles into him. While that fellow in the peak cap stood at the foot of the bed nodding his approval.

Then there was Mr Reade and his grandfather and Daisy . . . and his granny. Oh, he mustn't forget his granny. The man in the peak cap seemed to know his granny an' all, for he danced round her while making faces at her. It was a very strange experience, but one minute he was watching the man dancing round his granny and expressing his opinion of her with his grimaces, and the next minute it was himself who was dancing round her, and he was sticking his tongue out at her as far as it would go. Eeh! by! if she had seen him his life wouldn't have been worth living.

... That was funny, everybody was talking about his life and being worth living, being worth saving. But he didn't want to live. There was a reason why he didn't want to live, and he tried to tell himself the reason, but he couldn't, until he thought he saw his mother sitting by the bed. And then he knew the reason. He couldn't face her and see the look in her eyes when she told him he had fallen down on the job. All she had asked him to do was to see to Penny. And where was Penny now?

'Penny! Penny!'

'It's all right, dear, Penny's here. Look, she's got a hold of your hand.'

It took him a long time before he could open his eyes because somebody had put gum on his lids.

'Open your eyes, dear.'

'Ma.'

'Yes, my dear, you're all right ... you're all right. Lie quiet.'

He lay quiet for a while until there penetrated through his mind lines of pain. They were radiating from his arm, his hand, his chest, in fact all his body seemed a mass of pain.

'Ma.'

'Yes, dear?'

'I'm sore.'

'Yes, I know you are, dear, but you're getting better. Just drink this and then go to sleep.'

He gulped at the warm liquid from the spout of the feeding cup, and over its rim he blinked up into the face of his mother ... What was she doing here? What was the matter with him anyway? And where had everybody gone? The room had been full of people a minute ago, people he knew, and people he didn't know. And where was that fellow in the peak cap?

'Go to sleep, dear.'

He didn't want to go to sleep again because then that fellow would take over and there they would go careering up and down that passage, jumping that terrifying hole, racing over the beach to the edge of the waves and cutting the candles open. Aye. His mind groped at the last thought. That's what he had been doing a minute ago, helping that bloke to cut all the candles open and pull out the twine. *Why*? *Why*?

'Go to sleep, lad.'

He made an attempt to open his eyes wider. That was his granny's voice. Oh, his granny! He couldn't stand his granny. Well, he'd pretend to go to sleep just to stop her from nagging him. The company of the fellow in the peak cap was preferable to that of his granny.

It seemed a lifetime later when, propped up on pillows, he looked on his mother in full recognition and said weakly, 'How did you get here, Ma?'

'Well' – she smiled at him – 'I came back the same way as I went, by train and tram.'

'Did they send for you?'

'They hadn't any need. I . . . I read the paper and I was on my way. I got in an hour after they brought you home.'

'How . . . how did they find me? An' . . . an' what happened to him, the Belgian? Did they get him?'

'Oh yes, they got him all right, dear. And thank God, they were just in time because . . . well, you'll never know, boy, how near you were to death. He intended to put an end to you. It was Ted Reade who saved your life . . . and Penny's.' She reached out and gripped her daughter's hand, and Penny who was sitting on the side of the bed hitched herself further up towards Eddie, only to be reprimanded by her mother, saying, 'Careful. Careful.'

'How . . . how did he know where I was?'

'Well, Ted tells me that the coastguards saw you running along the cliff top, and he himself was coming up from the shore where he had been searching yet once again, and he knowing a little bit about you realized that you wouldn't be running without a purpose and he says as much to the coastguard, and at that they turned back with him and followed the direction you had gone. And so came up to Biddy's. That's all there was to it.'

That's all there was to it. If the coastguard hadn't met up with Mr Reade that's all there would have been to it and he would have been dead by now and his ghost likely would have been scampering up and down that passage with that fellow. Funny, but he couldn't get that man out of his mind.

'Where have they got him, I mean the Belgian?'

'Where he will be safe for many years to come, and not only him, the captain of the boat that did the ferrying under the guise of carrying legitimate cargo, and his crew along with him.' She paused now and patted the hand that was unbandaged, saying, 'You did something, Eddie,

165

when you tackled that man, for the others were merely pawns. He was the organizer, the brains, the great deceiver, for from what I hear he had the manners and actions of a gentleman.'

He looked from his mother to Penny, then back to her again as he said, 'Did they get all the children?'

There was a pause before she answered, 'Yes, all of them this time; but there have been other cargoes that weren't so fortunate.'

It was Penny who broke the silence that followed. In a small voice, she said, 'You've been in all the papers, Eddie. They called you, "Young Dock Hero".'

'Young Dock Hero.' He didn't like the title, neither the word Dock nor Hero. He certainly didn't feel like any hero, and when that knife had gone into him . . . On the memory he went to draw a deep breath but found his chest restricted and, looking down at the bandages and his strapped arm, he asked now, 'How long am I going to be like this, Ma?'

'Oh, some little time I'm afraid, dear. You'll have to be patient.'

'But what about me job? I've lost two days already.'

He stared at her. It was good to see her laugh.

'You've lost more than two days, boy, more like ten altogether.'

'What!'

She nodded at him, then went on, 'As for your job, I don't think you need worry about that. In fact, I could say there will be many openings in the town for you if you have a mind to take them.'

'I don't want to take any other job but what I'm at now, as long as I end up as an engineer.'

'Well, you'll end up as an engineer all right. But there are quicker ways to it than working in the docks.'

'Quicker ways to what than working in the docks?'

His granny had come into the room and behind her, carrying a tray, was Daisy.

'What were you talking about, quicker ways than what?'

'He says he just wants to be an engineer, Ma.'

'Well, who's stopping him?' His granny was staring at him now. Her body, like a piece of thin wire, was bent towards him. Her unchanging face was on a level with his, and now she went on, 'There's nobody stopping you being an engineer, but you won't serve your time laying there being pampered, will you, and having the whole blooming house running after you, waiting on you hand and foot . . . You want to be an engineer. Then get yourself off that bed. But first of all eat this. Give it here, girl!' She grabbed the tray from Daisy, who was standing behind her, and, placing it on his knees in an action that was much gentler than her words, she added, 'And don't you dare leave a drop of that soup or you'll get it for your breakfast in the morning.'

Mrs Flannagan now straightened her back, flapped the palms of her hands against each other, then, looking across at her daughter, said, 'This place is like a mad house. Three of them downstairs demanding interviews. I'll interview them with my toe in their backsides. Interviews!' She

167

turned her gaze on Eddie again and repeated loudly, 'Interviews indeed!' and with that she marched from the room. Daisy followed her, but not before she hunched her shoulders up around her neck, poked out her head towards Eddie and bit on her lip.

The door closed, the room quiet again, Eddie looked from the appetizingly set tray to his mother, and when he was about to speak she put her hand out and touched his one good one, saying softly, 'She's in her element, she's happy. I've never seen her so happy for years.'

Happy! That was his granny happy? Well, if that was happiness you could keep it for him.

By! the quicker he got out of here the better. Oh, to be back home and on the job again, and mixing with people, normal people; people who laughed when they were happy, and were kind when they were happy, and didn't bellow like a bull when they were happy; people as unlike his granny as it was possible to imagine.

He paused in his thinking – perhaps she was happy because she'd apparently got part of her hearing back.

Oh, she was a puzzle to him. He wished he could understand her. He wished he could tell himself he liked her.

Huh! that would be the day when he told himself he liked his granny. It'd be such an event they'd have flags flying from all the ships on the river. Aye, right from Shields to Newcastle.

9

It was the middle of December. The snow was lying a foot thick all around the house and for once it seemed to have deadened the sound of the waves against the rocks.

Inside the house everything was warm and cheerful, especially in the parlour where, except for Daisy who was in the kitchen, the whole household sat before the blazing fire. Mr Reade was sitting with them.

Mr Flannagan sat in his usual high-backed chair to one side of the fireplace and Mrs Flannagan at the other. To Mr Flannagan's right Penny, her feet curled around her, was on the couch, with her mother next to her, and in the middle of the couch sat Ted Reade with Eddie on his right within an arm's length of his granny's chair.

They'd all had a fine tea, a birthday tea, for today was Mrs Flannagan's sixty-sixth birthday. And now she was about to do something that she had promised Eddie when in one of her rare softer moods. 'Some day,' she had said, 'when the time is ripe and we're all together, at least all those concerned, I'll tell you about that

169

man in the peak cap.' And so she had chosen the night of her birthday to explain the mystery of the man who haunted the passage, and the reason why the passage had been built at all.

'Well now' – she looked from one to the other – 'I know what you're all waiting for, you not least of all, Lily' – she pointed to her daughter – 'for you've been kept as much in the dark as I was when I was young. But when I finish telling my tale, which is no fairy tale but the gospel truth, you'll see the reason why we' – she indicated her husband with a flip of her hand – 'have kept mum about the passage all these years. And we will want you all here to do the same from now on.' She paused. 'But we're not all here are we? Where's that Daisy? Get off your perch, boy, and go and fetch her. You know' – she nodded round the company – 'he's getting as lazy as he's long; he's living on his past glory. He is. He is.'

'Aw, Gran!' Eddie got to his feet, indignation in his tone. 'I've been wanting to go back to work for . . .'

'Now none of your old lip and go about your business and fetch her in.'

As Eddie went out of the sitting room into the hall the sound of laughter followed him and his chin jerked. Aw, his granny!

In the kitchen Daisy was busy putting away the last of the crockery and she turned and looked at him and said, 'If you've come to give a hand you're too late.'

'That'll be the day,' he said, grinning at her.

'Aye, I dare say it will.' She grinned back at him.

'Me granny says you've got to come in. She's gona tell us about the passage an' why it was built.'

'Oh! Oh, good. But I've got to finish here first and tidy meself up.'

'Never mind that. Come on!' Impulsively he reached out and grabbed her hand. 'She's in full cry the night and she'll eat us alive if we don't get back.'

'But eeh! look, I'm not tidy for the sittin' room.'

He now pressed his head back and looked her up and down, then said airily, 'You look all right to me . . . Aw, come on.'

She allowed him to pull her up the kitchen, but as they entered the dim hall she drew him to a stop and stood peering up at him for a moment before she whispered, 'I've never thanked you, Eddie, for what you did for me. Eeh! I lie awake at nights and shiver an' think what might have become of me if you hadn't been there.'

'Aw' – he moved his head from side to side – 'if it hadn't been me that put a spoke in their wheel, somebody else would have, like Mr Reade or the coastguard . . . And anyway, they did more than their share to bring things to a head. Oh aye, if it hadn't been for Mr Reade I wouldn't be standin' here nattering to you. Now would I?'

'No, I daresay not.' She was whispering up at him again.

'But it was you who came down to the cove and got me; the missis could never have done it on her own.'

171

Her eyes were large, her face was bright. He stared down into it; then the next moment he almost toppled backwards as her arms came round his neck and her mouth fell full on his.

He didn't remember how his hands had got on each side of her waist but when he realized he was holding her he didn't draw away. He knew that he was red up to the ears and he wanted to take in a deep breath. He did so, and as he let it out, he said, 'By! you're a cheeky monkey.'

'Aye, I know.' She was laughing at him now.

'You want your lug skelped.'

'Aye, I know.'

'And one of these days I'll skelp it for you . . . you'll see.'

'I'll look forward to that.'

'Eeh! By! . . . Aw, come on.' He grabbed her hand again yet didn't move immediately; but what he did next took more courage then he had needed to go up the dark stairs of Biddy McMann's cottage, for now he leaned quickly forward and kissed her on the cheek. Then he almost lifted her off her feet as he spurted across the hall and only in time pulled them up at the sitting room door. Here, dropping her hand, he aimed at adopting a nonchalant attitude, but when he saw the look on her face he bent down to her and hissed, 'Don't look like that or she'll twig.'

For answer Daisy pursed her mouth, moved it round and round, then stretched her upper lip away from her nose, widened her eyes and attempted to get her expression back to something like normal; but what she succeeded in doing was to make Eddie clap his hands across

172

his mouth and bite tight on his lip to stop himself from laughing outright.

Then turning from her, he stared at the blank face of the door for a moment before thrusting it open and marching into the room.

'You've taken your time, where've you been? Doing another rescue?'

'Aw, Gran.' He wished he could think of something else to say but, Aw, Gran, yet if he dared to say to her what was in his mind he would no doubt have to make a run for it.

He now pushed Daisy past his grandmother and on to the sofa next to Mr Reade; then he resumed his own seat and made himself return his grandmother's stare. She was looking right through him. Had she twigged what had happened out in the hall? He wouldn't put it past her; she was a witch.

Slowly she took her gaze from him and settled herself back in her chair, then said, 'Now, here I go, and I'll start at the beginning as I know it. When my grandfather was a boy . . .

'Well, his name was Benjamin McAlister and he was brought up along the coast there when Shields was little more than a fishing village, that was in 1770. His own father had been drowned off the sands, together with his two elder brothers, and his mother was determined that the sea wouldn't get the only one she had left, so when me grandfather was but nine years old she apprenticed him to a stonemason. One of his first jobs was to lead the horse that carried the slabs from the quarry. Eventually he gravitated to the yard itself, and from sweeping up he learned to chip and rub, and as he did so there grew in him a love of the stone; so much so that he promised himself that one day he'd build his own house of it. Yet he knew that was a big-headed ambition for a lad who was earning a shilling a week.

'Now in his spare time, but mostly on a Sunday, he walked these cliffs and the beach down there. And one night, it was in the height of the summer time and a new moon was coming up, and it was a rare night for these parts for it was so hot he couldn't sleep indoors, so he wandered out and right along the coast here. And when he turned the point where the rock juts out just down below' – she thumbed towards the window now – 'what did he make out but four dim figures treading back and forward in the water unloading a boat. Now at the sight of them he froze and pressed himself against the rocks because there were some nasty customers went in for smuggling in those days. Well, they had to be men of a certain calibre because once caught it could be a long stretch, or even transportation.

'Well, as he stood watching them, petrified with fright, the whole bunch of them stopped what they were doing, then slowly as if taking a walk they moved along the edge of the tide until they were within a few yards of him. Then like wild animals they collared him, and it was only by one of the men letting out an oath that he saved his skin, for he recognized the gruff Scottish tones of the cutter whom he worked under and he yelled out, "Mr Brady! Mr Brady!"

'The four of them now stood over him where he lay cowering on the sand, and it was the man,

Brady, who said, "Why, it's young Ben McAlister. God! boy, what are you doin' here?" and he answered truthfully, "Taking a jaunt, Mr Brady, 'cos I felt stuffed up inside."

'The men now moved away and had a confab, and when they came back it was Mr Brady who said, "Well, now you're here, lad, you might as well give a hand," and of course with that he became one of them. Whether he liked it or not he became one of them. And he did like it. Oh aye, he liked it. He never stopped being afraid, so I'm told, because that would have been foolish, it's only fools who say they have no fear, but from that night he looked upon his adventure as being God-given, for now he could see whereby he could get the means to one day build his stone house.

'So time went on and he became a fine stone-mason and long before he was twenty he had helped to build a number of houses roundabout. It was when he was twenty-four that he took a most important step and he married Mat Brady's daughter, Amy.

'Now Amy was three years older than him, and a big fine strapping lass, and she, too, had ideas about a house, their own house. But as with him it was a dream to be worked for. And work they did, for years, right up to 1810, by which time they had two sons, Joe who was now fifteen, and Dan who was fourteen.

'Anyway, it was one night in 1810 when she was helping to unload a special cargo on the coast down there and the weather was more than rough that they took shelter in the cave for a while. Now she had been in that cave countless times before,

175

as had me grandfather and the other men, and they always made a point of seeing that they left nothing behind that might give prying coast-guards a lead, but when she got back home that particular night she realized to her dismay that she had left her neck shawl in the cave. She had been soaked through and she had taken her coat off and the shawl; then because something caused the men to be uneasy, they had, according to plan, scattered in various directions, and she, in her hurry, had forgotten the shawl. So away she goes back the next morning, and there's the shawl lying where she had left it.

'The rain had stopped and the sun was out, and as is often the case after a night of rain the light appeared clearer. And as she looked at the early sun striking a part of the wall just inside the entrance she realized that only for a very short time in the day would even the entrance to the cave see any sun. So she stands and sort of admires the effect, then she walks to the far wall, and on looking up she sees a hole a few feet above her head.

'Now it was only a small hole, about a foot and a half wide, more like a deep fissure, but it intrigued her somehow, stirred her curiosity like. So what does she go and do but gather some rocks and pile them one on top of the other until she could stand on them and bring her head and shoulders level with the hole. And when she pushed her head through, what did she see? Nothing, because it was black dark. But she got the feeling of space and she also got an excited feeling in the pit of her stomach.

176

'Anyway, she can do nothing on her own, so back home she goes, and when her husband, me grandfather you know, came in at dinnertime for his meal she tells him about her discovery, and she says, "We'll take a lantern, Ben, and we'll get in there. I think we're on to something. Just imagine if there was a cave there an' you could make that hole big enough to pass the stuff through instead of risking carting it along the coast, camouflaged in all shapes and sizes. Why, if we could store it there, we could hoodwink the whole coastguards from here to Hull, and the militia into the bargain."

'By the way' – Mrs Flannagan now nodded from one to the other – 'it was mostly baccy and brandy and silks and choice stuff like that they dealt in.

'So later that day they take a lantern and they go back to the cave and me grandfather bunks her up, but she has a job to get through and so has he. Anyway, when they get up from their knees and hold the lantern aloft, what do they see but a fine big space, a cave within a cave, airy and dry. And what do they do? Their eyes meet in glee; me granny puts the lantern down, and they throw their arms about each other.'

Here Mrs Flannagan stopped the narrative and laughed to herself. Then turning to Ted Reade, she said, 'Get on your pins, Ted, and pour us out a drink, talking's thirsty work. Ginger beer for these three.' She flapped her hand in the direction of the couch, then sat back in her chair.

A few minutes later they all had glasses in their hands and when Eddie almost finished his drink at one go, his granny cried at him, 'You've got a mouth like a sink, boy! Don't you ever take to anything stronger or you'll spend your life lying on the floor.'

They all laughed at Eddie's expense, but he refrained from answering, not even to say to himself, 'Aw! me granny.' He just stared at her and waited impatiently for her to go on. And now she did.

'Well, following the discovery of the cave within the cave, so to speak, me granny's mind started to work overtime.

' "About the house you're going to build," she said to me grandfather one day. "I've found the very place for it." So she brought him along the cliff top here, and she pointed out the site which was in a direct line from the cave but well above the slope. At first he thought she was mad. Build a house this far from the town, and wide open to the wind and weather, the sea on the doorstep, what was she thinking about! It was different back in the town. There the huddled houses sheltered each other. No, it was a mad idea.

'But me granny stuck to her guns. And then she pointed out something to him that had been in her mind all the time but was news to him. "That inner cave down there," she said, "could be connected with the house and nobody would know a thing about it but ourselves. And as you know, the others say they are going to give up here because this quarter's getting too hot for them. The watchdogs are getting fly. So before long they'll take the run farther along the coast."

'Me grandfather, so I'm told, looked at his wife

and again he threw his arms about her. Of course, I don't think either of them would have been so merry at that moment if they had known that there was ten years of hard slogging afore them.

'Anyway, there it is. Me grandfather and grandmother, with the help of my father Joe and his brother Dan, started to build this house from plans that me grandmother had drawn up. A rough plan, but a clever one nevertheless, for if you measure the inside of the house you'll find it all of eight feet short of the outside, and if you measure the width you'll find it two foot less in the inside from where my bedroom begins to where it ends.

'As I've said me grandfather was a stone-mason, he could make two pieces of stone meet as if they had never been split. He could make a stone swivel like an oiled hinge. They worked every spare minute they had on the house for three years. People came out and had a look at it. "What thick walls you are building!" they said. "But you'll need them with the sea at your door." "What's those long narrow rooms on the end for?" they said. "Oh, they're going to be a couple of storerooms and a water closet."

' "What! a water closet?" They laughed their heads off at that. Aping the gentry, they said. A water closet, and all the coast line to do your business on. It was daft. Anyway, the house seemed such a long time going up that people lost interest in it.

'But at last it was finished and me grandparents and their two sons took up their abode here. There wasn't much furniture at first

179

because they had spent nearly all they had on stones and wood.

'And then began the real work, which they did mostly at night. It was nothing to them making the false door from the bedroom into the cavity wall. It was when they began to break into the rock foundation below that they realized what kind of a task they had set themselves. But they went at it inch by inch, foot by foot, year after year.

'In the meantime the cave above the cave had come in more than handy. But there was always the fear that someone with an eye as sharp as me granny's would look up one morning and see the hole and investigate. They did think about putting a stone door there but then that would have meant having a lever on the outside.

'So there was nothing for it but to go on chiselling downwards. Sometimes they went too steeply, sometimes not steep enough, which made them drop the next grade steeper still. Then one night they were brought to a full stop for they came on a shelf of rock where the grain wouldn't give way to either hammer or chisel, it needed an explosive, and that, of course, was out of the question. So it took them months to make a way through that single point. And that's the part where a woman with an outsize bust or a man with a pot belly would come unstuck.'

When the laughter died down, she continued, 'Down and down they went, and then one night their chisel goes straight through the rock as if through a thin layer of paper. It was me father who was chiselling at the time and he quickly makes a hole big enough for his head, his hand and a candle, and what he saw I'm told, and I believe him, because it's had the same effect on me, turned his blood cold for he was looking down into the dark roaring depth of a cleft and the sound was deafening.

'One after the other they took their turns in looking through the hole, and the lads, that was me father and me uncle Dan, were for giving up. Even me grandfather thought, well, that was the end, but not me granny. Oh no. "We'll go round it," she said. "After all, what is it but a cleft in the rock. It's a wonder we haven't come across one afore now. We'll skirt it with a loop."

'My father told me from his own lips that me grandfather's hair turned snow white during the six months of nights it took them to chisel their way round that hole. But once beyond it they all worked like maniacs because they knew that now they were within yards of their goal.

'But what nearly drove them all white-haired was the night that they actually broke through. So elated were they, they were just about to jig and dance when they heard voices which froze them all into statues. Fortunately they weren't coming from the cave but from outside on the shore. They never knew whose voices they were, whether coastguards, or polis, or mates in the same game as their own, but they stayed frozen until the sound of the voices died away. Then cautiously they went back up the long trek and came into the house, and once inside they did jig, they did laugh . . . and they did get drunk, blind, mortallious.

'Would you mind filling the glasses again, Ted?'

'Aye, Maggie. And I think I'll have a long one, something cooling because you've got the sweat running down me oxters. You have that.'

'You, Daisy, get up off your backside and give Mr Reade a hand.'

'Aye, missis. Aye, missis.' Daisy seemed to have to pull herself up as if out of a dream.

As for Eddie, he leant against the head of the couch and looked about him. Everybody, he saw, was sweating; but, of course, it could be the fire, it was blazing high.

When his mother leant across the couch and touched his hand he gripped her fingers and smiled at her. But, of course, his granny had to go and spoil it by crying, 'That's it, treat him like a bairn. Hasn't he been spoilt enough these past weeks?'

His mother didn't answer his granny but she continued to smile at him and pressed his fingers more tightly before releasing her hold on them.

Mrs Flannagan now called to Daisy, saying, 'And bring those plates. I think we could do with somethin' to eat an' all.'

'Oh, Mother!' Lilian was leaning forward now. 'Let's wait; I want to hear the end, we all do.'

'Oh well, just as you say.'

It was odd, Eddie thought as he drank his ginger beer, that his granny's tone when speaking to her daughter could be so different from the one she used when speaking to him. But here she was going again.

'As you know,' she was saying, 'it's local his-

182

tory the boats that have been wrecked along this coast, and not a few, if all the truth were told, were scuttled on purpose. Well, about this particular time I'm coming to, me father was around twenty-five years old and me Uncle Dan twenty-four. Me father had joined me grandfather early on in the mason's yard but not me Uncle Dan; he took after his own grandfather so he went out with the fishing boats. And, of course, this in a way was a good thing for the business they had on the side, for it was a kind of blind. By this time, too, me Uncle Dan had his own little boat. He was the kind of man that must always be his own master, and, as I also understand, he was as different from me father as chalk was from cheese 'cos he was wild in his ways and drank heavily, whereas although me granda and me father liked their drop they knew when to stop. But not me Uncle Dan.

'Anyway, it was around this time, as I said, that me Uncle Dan got very mysterious and talked about big pickings, and one night when the weather was bad, real wild, he tells them all, me granny included, to get down to the top cave, that's what they called the one where the candles are now, and wait for a signal from him. By now me grandfather had fitted a door in the aperture of the cave, but it could only be opened from the inside.

'Anyway, there they were, me grandfather, me grandmother and me father waiting. And then the signal comes and they open the door, and there down below is me Uncle Dan standing knee deep in water. And he's nearly bursting with excitement, and bobbing all around him are long boxes. "Get them up! Get them up!" he shouts, and they haul the boxes one after another into the upper cave. And still they come. Even when the water's swirling round his waist, he guides more and more boxes from outside the cave to the foot of the rope ladder, and they all work until their arms are fit to drop off and until there's hardly room to move on the floor of the cave. Not until the water reached his chin and the last box was up the ladder, would me Uncle Dan come up. And you know what he did then? He lay down on the floor of the cave and laughed until the tears rolled down his face. And they laughed with him although they didn't know what they were laughing at. Then springing to his feet, he attacked the first box to his hand with an axe, and when it burst open they stood amazed as candles rippled out onto their feet.

' "Candles?" me grandfather cried. "What in the name of God is this!"

' "You wait," cried me Uncle Dan. "You wait. Did you bring the knives with you?"

' "Aye." They all nodded at him.

' "Well, get going then and split them up."

' "Split the candles up? What in the name of God for?" me granny now cried at him.

' "Because, dear Ma," he said, "there's a fortune hidden in these here candles that's going to make me rich and you rich; and you, Da, rich; and you, our cautious Joe, make you rich an' all. Rich as Lords, all of us."

'So without asking any more questions they all started splitting the candles like madmen, and

184

they went on splitting the candles all night until they were almost buried in candle tallow and tallowed string; but still there were more boxes to go through.

'It was me granny who called a final halt. "There's another day," she said. "There's another day." And Dan, weary himself now, said, "Aye, you're right, Ma."

'So back to the house they came, and me Uncle Dan answering their demands to know what it was all about explained to them that quite by accident he had found out that the shipment of candles was a blind. It was a comparatively small boat, hardly much bigger than a wherry, but it was laden to the water mark and it was making for Hull where it was to pass its cargo on to a bigger ship there.

'It was at this point that the business got nasty, for me grandfather gripping his son by the throat, demanded, "Tell me, you had no hand in the scuttlin'?" and although me Uncle Dan denied it with angry curses me grandfather didn't believe him; nor did me grandma, nor me father.

' "How did it get so near inshore? they demanded."

' "Because," Dan said, "it was blown off course by the storm."

' "What about the men on board?"

' "They had got away in a sculler," he said.

' "Then it was a put-up job," me granny accused him.

'No. Yes. No. He waffled, and kept protesting that he'd had no hand in the scuttling and it was

185

the small crew that had thought the whole thing up.

'Anyway, the next day when he went down through the passage to start splitting the candles again he went alone.

'Now at different times when Dan had been passing up and down the passage he had, the dare-devil that he was, despised going round the loop and had jumped the hole, and more than once me granny's heart had leapt into her throat. If he had drink on him and the devil in him he would dance round the hole.

'Well, when he had been down in the upper cave nearly all day, me granny decided to take him something to eat, and it was as she edged her way through the narrow cleft that she heard his whoops of joy and she knew that he had found what he was after. She also knew that the sound was coming not from the upper cave but from near the crevasse.

'It was a mild day outside and the sea demons in the hole were strangely quiet, and so when the passage suddenly rang with an ear-splitting, fearful, piercing scream she turned her face to the rock wall and banged her head against it, after which she became strangely still. When she turned about it was not in the direction of the crevasse but up towards the house, and when me grandfather came in he found her sitting near the open stone door in the bedroom.

'When he demanded to know what had happened she didn't speak but she pointed into the passage. He went in and down, and after a time he came out again and looked at her, but still she didn't speak.

'Me father had arrived home by now and he and

me granda went down past the loop to the candle room, as it came to be called. The place looked like something you would imagine at the bottom of the sea, broken white wax and hundreds of pieces of string, seemingly mountains of it, with splintered crates sticking up out of them like ribs of dead ships. But there was no sign of me Uncle Dan. Apparently he had found what he was looking for and it had gone with him.'

Mrs Flannagan's voice was low now as she said, 'It was four days later when his body was washed ashore. Me granny lived for another two years after that but she rarely spoke unless it was absolutely necessary, so me father said.

'Well, me grandfather was not long in following her, a year to be exact. And there was me father left alone and lonely. So he lets another year go by out of respect and then he marries. That was early in 1824 and I was born here the same year. And here I grew up. But I knew nothing about the wall room, the passage or anything else until I was well into womanhood.

'So' – she now turned and addressed Eddie – 'you know now, lad, who the man was in the peak cap and the reefer jacket. But you're not the first one he's guided aright in dreams, as old Doctor Collington knows, but guide you he did, I'm sure of that, for I would never have gone back down there that morning if you hadn't mentioned what you called your nightmare.'

Mrs Flannagan now did an unusual thing, at least to Eddie it was unusual for, leaning towards him, she patted him on the knee and the pat had an affectionate touch about it. So much so that he thought, wonders will never cease; I'd better have another nightmare the night. But no; he mustn't joke about the nightmares. Whatever good that fellow had done, he didn't want to see him again, sleeping or waking.

They all now remained still and silent for a moment as his granny said softly, 'The only thing I hope is we'll never have to use that passage again. You know, I used to hate it at one time, but not anymore, not since it was the means of saving my man. But then, that only came about by the sharp eyes of me grandson.' She now actually caused the colour to flood up to the roots of Eddie's hair as she added, 'And not only did he do that but he saved his sister and brought an evil man to justice, and narrowly escaped with his life in doing so. And . . .'

'And he came down and got me, missis.'

All eyes were now turned on Daisy, and Mrs Flannagan, nodding at her, said briskly, 'You'll never forget that till the day you die, will you?'

'No, I won't that, missis, never till the day I die.' Daisy was not smiling anymore and Mrs Flannagan nodded at her and said, 'Well, that's as it should be.' But now she was looking at Eddie again, and her voice unusually soft, she said, 'He and I know there's somebody else we should thank, don't we, lad? The man in the peak cap who haunted your dreams. We should thank him, shouldn't we, lad?'

'Aye, Gran.'

'I doubt if you hadn't told me about him if we'd ever have gone down there again that night. Aye, I doubt it very much. But there, we did, didn't we?' Again she was gripping his knee. 'And he led us to Hal Kemp. And you fought him like a man. Aye. Aye, you did that. I reckon I was as proud of you as I've been of anybody in me life as I looked down on you bashing away at that creature. And when later I had time to meself to think, do you know what I thought, lad?'

It was as if they were alone in the room together now, facing each other, quite unaware of those around them, and he answered her softly, 'No, Gran.'

'Well, lad, I thought, he comes of good stock on both sides; it's as he said, his father was a good man. And I say now to your face, and to me daughter's' – she flicked her eyes in the direction of Lilian – 'I wish I'd realized it earlier, for me own sake, as well as everybody else's.' . . .

'Aw, Gran!' Simultaneously their arms went out, and about each other, and he felt the strength of her small frame as he hugged her to him, and for the second time in one evening he was kissed full on the mouth. But before he had time to savour the miracle he was pushed forcibly from her and she was bawling at him in her own inimitable way, 'And if ever I hear you calling me Gran-Flan again I'll swipe the hunger off you! Do you hear me?'

'I hear you, Gran-Flan.'

The room was alive with laughter, his mother's mixed with tears, his granny's high and cracking to cover her emotion, his grandfather's deep and throaty, Penny's a high pipe, Daisy's merry and gurgling, Ted's a choking chuckle. There was only himself in all the company that wasn't laughing aloud.

He was sitting back on the couch, his arm outstretched still holding his granny's hand, and the feeling inside him couldn't be expressed through laughter. He was filled with a strange happiness, a complete and bewildering happiness, and he realized in this moment that he had never felt so secure and safe in all his life. He also realized that his mind was confronting him with a problem, for it was asking, 'How was it possible to love somebody that you once hated?' for now he knew he loved his Granny Flannagan.

THE END

OUR JOHN WILLIE
by Catherine Cookson

Our John Willie helps his older brother, Davy,
to escape from the dreadful mining disaster.
But their father is killed in the accident and
Davy knows that it is now up to him to take care
of his brother – not an easy task since John
Willie has been deaf and dumb since birth.

Out on the road with nowhere to go, life looks
very grim indeed for the two boys, until
eccentric, sharp-tongued Miss Peamarsh takes
a hand, offering them a bright new future. But
then Davy stumbles across a horrifying secret
from Miss Peamarsh's past – a secret that could
destroy their new-found happiness . . .

A strong and heartwarming story, set in the
rough but sympathetic world of mining life in
the northeast.

0 552 525251

CORGI

If you would like to receive a Newsletter about our new Children's books, just fill in the coupon below with your name and address (or copy it onto a separate piece of paper if you don't want to spoil your book) and send it to:

The Children's Books Editor
Transworld Publishers Ltd.
61–63 Uxbridge Road,
Ealing
London W5 5SA

Please send me a Children's Newsletter:

Name: ....

Address: ....

....

....

All Children's Books are available at your bookshop or newsagent, or can be ordered from the following address:
Corgi/Bantam Books,
Cash Sales Department,
P.O. Box 11, Falmouth, Cornwall TR10 9EN

Please send a cheque or postal order (no currency) and allow 60p for postage and packing for the first book plus 25p for the second book and 15p for each additional book ordered up to a maximum charge of £1.90 in UK.

B.F.P.O. customers please allow 60p for the first book, 25p for the second book plus 15p per copy for the next 7 books, thereafter 9p per book.

Overseas customers, including Eire, please allow £1.25 for postage and packing for the first book, 75p for the second book, and 28p for each subsequent title ordered.